RUPERT:

A CONFESSION

ILJA LEONARD PFEIJFFER

RUPERT:
A CONFESSION

TRANSLATED FROM THE DUTCH
BY MICHELE HUTCHISON

OPEN LETTER
LITERARY TRANSLATIONS FROM THE UNIVERSITY OF ROCHESTER

Library of Congress Control Number: 2009902468
ISBN-13: 978-1-934824-09-2 / ISBN-10: 1-934824-09-7

Publication of this novel has been made possible with the financial support from
the Foundation for Production and Translation of Dutch Literature.

Printed on acid-free paper in the United States of America.

Text set in Garamond, an old-style serif typeface named for the punch-cutter
Claude Garamond (c. 1480-1561).

Design by N. J. Furl

Open Letter is the University of Rochester's nonprofit, literary translation press:
Lattimore Hall 411, Box 270082, Rochester, NY 14627

www.openletterbooks.org

CONTENTS

THE FIRST HEARING

1 A disappointing kind of sun was shining. She lures you outside with her radiant eyes and blackmails you with the accusation that you're missing some exceptional, lovely weather, but once you've gone outside, full of good intentions, and you're walking the streets, along with all those other cheery city-dwellers and tourists blinking with confusion, you wished you'd put on a thicker sweater. But to go back now would be an affront to the beautiful day—lovely weather really, mustn't grumble, pity to stay indoors. And besides, I didn't know what to do at home. It was Sunday.

I set off in my usual direction. The afternoon you've decided to wander aimlessly through the city is not the afternoon to deviate from your habitual route. That's not something I like to do in general. I'd rather reread the proper streets, squares, and cafés than run the risk of wasting my time in a neighborhood whose scenery, poor style, and a lack of interesting characters might bore me, and just because I'd succumbed to some adventurous longing. If, God forbid, this were a novel of ideas rather than the erstwhile account of the deed, that I, members of the jury, am explaining to you without roses, perfume, or gold-leaf, I'd insert an appropriate aphorism, such as: in everything, except love, the attractions of the unknown are terribly overestimated. Or, it is better to revisit than visit a place. Or perhaps even: walking is a form of remembering. Although I presumed to lay claim to these and other such deep insights on occasion during such Sunday perambulations, it would demonstrate little rhetorical awareness if, in my present situation, I brought my powers of judgment into my plea before this court.

And thus, on the aforementioned Sunday afternoon, April 13th, a radiant spring day, I, Rupert the Rightly, walked past Alkala station along Concordia Avenue, into town, towards Fredoplein with no deep thoughts, plans, or having passed judgment on anything whatsoever. My shadow ambled along after me. As to the pace at which I was walking, I can tell you that it was a proper pace. I walked as I like to walk, in a steady, dignified manner, without appearing tardy: like a high-ranking Italian carabiniere with a gleaming, polished belt buckle walking the beat in his home village. A man who wouldn't miss even the most inconsequential-looking sign of impending doom or moral ruin but who can happily confirm that, thanks to his vigilant and attentive eye, things are, for the time being, completely as they should be. Because that's how it was. The twenty-four hour shops on Concordia Avenue were open. The shoppers were husbands and wives, couples, girlfriends, women, and mothers with children. They went into the shops and came right out again with bags from the various life-style temples and other similar confessions. On they went, grown accustomed to believing in a cut-price paradise in which individuals distinguish themselves by the repeated purchase of whichever logos are all the rage again in the right circles. Buses regularly refreshed the supply of devotees. The stairs to the metro presented people ascending or descending at different speeds. Many, so many. I had not thought death had undone so many. Each one with eyes fixed to the ground in front of his feet. Chestnut-sellers sold chestnuts. Porn was displayed on the most prominent shelves of the newspaper kiosks, cellophane-wrapped with yellow stickers covering the nipples and pubic hair. Some covers were composed entirely of yellow stickers. Beggars were nicely begging. Street musicians played guitar, or just happened to be taking a break. Here and there a sniveling child was being told off. Taxis honked, and not only taxis. The benches along the pavement were rarely occupied, but when they were it was by elderly ladies with heavy bags who had the right to sit there.

I know this city. I know her moods, her curves, her smells. I know her quirks and habits, her tastes and her scornful silences. I know her warm, messy sluggishness when she doesn't want to get up in the morning, her ravishing, impromptu presence in the afternoon, her conversations between mirrors in her sparklingly-decorated, favorite local, and her dangerously seductive flirtations after sunset. I've kissed, stroked, tasted, and smoked every part, nook, dip, bone, muscle, and tendon of her shifting, transforming body. I know how she loiters in the Rivelath arcades, around the buzzing terraces of 1818 Square, and I know her expression when she's serving coffee in The Corona di Mócani. I know the drunken wind that blows through her hair on a late summer's evening when she's walking with her girlfriends along the old harbor to one of the smoky cinemas in the Latin Quarter, and I know the smell of rain on her jacket when she's forgotten her umbrella. I've seen her in a car, kissing at a traffic light, and weeping in the metro during the morning rush hour, a German book under her arm. I've seen her order a pancake with cream from a street-seller and scrape the cream off into a trash can on the next corner. I've seen her standing in sour-smelling alleyways with broken street lamps, late, at implausible hours, with lacquered loins of loss and a look of melting ice. Unreal city. I see her, remember her, and invent her. I'd know her from thousands.

"Excuse me, sir?" I could see he wasn't a beggar or a drug dealer. And certainly not the type with the nerve to ask for a cigarette and can you make it two. I don't know why they always go for me. I'm constantly approached in the street by the foulest scum. They certainly don't do it because they take me for the apathetic type, someone who will give in to being importuned. That would mean that every single one of them had misjudged me, and they wouldn't do that, because sizing up victims is their gift. They probably recognize me as a free soul, and in that respect, one of their own. They take my dignified pace and candid mien as a sign of open-minded nobility. I'm not one of those hurrying, neurotic citizens who brushes off or ignores his fellow men. I'm calm, noble, and courageous. I'm not afraid of beggars and scroungers, and I always give them something.

But this was a man was of a different caliber; I spot that kind of thing instantly. Although, I must say that he didn't look ordinary, with his short, baggy anorak, his sandals, and his Stetson bowler, idiotically decorated with two feathers, one on the right and the other on the left. He carried a walking stick, its handle a figure eight with the top section missing.

He carried the stick, I said, and that is the right expression, for he held it nonchalantly by the handle without putting any weight on it.

"Excuse me, sir? Way to U-stations please?" Whenever anyone asks me for directions I'm happy, for their sake, that that they've happened on to me. Giving directions to strangers is an art that few master. It requires, like any art, special skills and talents, and many people underestimate it. To start with, it is of the utmost importance that you know yourself how to get to the place they're looking for. You don't just need to know how to locate the required destination, but you also need to be able to visualize the route or various routes to it. You must run through the alternate routes in your mind, look for noticeable monuments or other landmarks, just as, when reciting from memory, you retain the main points of an argument by following a path along the principal points. At the same time, you should make a comparative assessment of the various options and select the most suitable route. This is not by definition the shortest. The lost pedestrian is less interested in speed than simplicity. The best route is the one that can be most easily described. This brings us to the most crucial and undervalued aspect of the act of giving directions: pedagogy. Most people begin gesticulating wildly and throw in irrelevant details, and the poor pedestrian has already lost the plot by the third alley. Directions should be given the way one elucidates a complex problem for a group of students. First, one should give a brief outline. One does that with a short and clear explanation of the current position, where the desired location is in relation to the current position, and what one's general orientation ought therefore to be. Along with this, one also gives an indication of the total distance to be covered. Only once the interlocutor has fully understood the basic points should one move on to a practical explanation of the route to follow. One should also refrain from giving too many details at this juncture, only relating what is strictly necessary. Naturally, one must have a thorough knowledge of all the details to determine what is useful for the argument and what is unnecessarily confusing. Thus, for example, one can only permit oneself to suggest that the traveler continues to the traffic lights if one is certain that there are no other traffic lights along the route to the intended intersection. Furthermore, choosing signs and landmarks that are easily memorized is of great importance. It is an example of lousy direction-giving to say: left at the third set of traffic lights, then right at the second set of traffic lights, and next left at the third set of traffic lights. The high art of direction-giving gives preference to unorthodox landmarks which stick immediately in the mind. For example: go straight until you see the word "Donkyman." Then turn left, given that all donkeys are left-legged. Carry on until you see a building that is so ugly it gives you a fright. Naturally, you don't want to go there, so you turn right, however much you might want to turn right around. There, you'll take an avenue that is bordered with plane trees. You'll feel you're in Aix-en-Provence, so it makes sense to continue until the smell of *coq au vin* and *entrecôte aux herbes provençales* reaches you from Le Lapin Gras bistro, which has those dishes on its menu this week. If you can resist temptation at this point and choose the narrow, less-traveled path on the right towards eternity, instead of the large road on the left towards the sensory delights, you'll be able to make out the cathedral at the end.

"U-stations?"

"The cathedral, yes. Saint Eustatius cathedral."

"Thank you very kind, sir. Can I have cigarette, sir, please?" No cigarettes, I've got roll ups. Would a roll up be alright? Roll up alright, but make it please because can't roll. Fine, I'll roll you one. Would you like to lick it yourself? No, not lick yourself? Fine, I'll lick. Here, you're welcome. "Can I have two, sir, please?" With an expression that exuded self-control—a self-control that was the fruit of years spent mastering a secret, lethal martial art—I silently rolled a second cigarette for him. He thanked me hastily and walked off in the right direction. But suddenly he turned around and shouted something in his stilted tourist's English. Then he made a face to accompany this, an oyea-oyea-oyea, watch out, important, important face, as if he'd suddenly had a moment of metaphysical enlightenment or a revelation of the secret decree of the Olympic gods, but I couldn't understand him. I nodded, but only to get rid of him. Luckily, he carried on. He walked extraordinarily quickly, he seemed almost to fly, and before I knew it he'd disappeared from sight.

2 ⁄ Members of the jury, I hope you will permit me to take a side-street at this point, one that might deviate from the shortest route to our destination, that dark, doomed alley in the Minair district where I committed my crime, or alleged crime, but one that takes us along a route that will give us some important intelligence about my case. At the end of the day, nothing less than my credibility is at stake. I want to raise the question of the reliability of my memory of the tragic events of April 13th, and I hope to convince you that you can trust my memory, which should greatly simplify your decision-making process.

He who must do without notes and give an address from memory (such as I am doing at the present moment) employs certain techniques in order not to lose the thread of his argument. These techniques are part of the *ars memorativa*, the art of memory, described in many documents from antiquity. One of the most effective methods makes use of "mnemonic space." The orator memorizes his argument by picturing a city he knows well. He imagines walking through the city along a route he's taken many times in real life, one which is rich in striking landmarks, such as monuments, public buildings, particular cafés, squares, fountains, libraries, or churches. These identifying features serve as *loci*, as *topoi*— common sites. During his mental journey, the orator runs through the main points of his argument and associates each point with a particular mnemonic site. Each episode of his story will be connected to a specific landmark on the selected route through the city. When the orator finally stands up to address the public, he has to do nothing more than take the same walk in his head as he speaks, picking up the points of his argument from the mnemonic sites he encounters on the way.

Writings from antiquity make mention of the importance of choosing the right mnemonic sites for the chief points of your speech. If the associations are completely random, the memory receives less assistance than if there is a logical, thematic connection between the place and the story. You shouldn't allow yourself to be attracted by striking locations as such, but by the meaning that these locations have. You shouldn't visit the city but read it. The old scriptures also recommend choosing the agora or forum as a mnemonic space: the political or religious heart of the city where laws are hewn in stone, where municipal decrees are set in marble, where temples of the gods are decorated with stories of avenging power, where there are monuments to fallen soldiers and triumphal arches that mark historic victories in battle. That's where the city can be read. Those places have meaning. The best orator is the one who is able to read out his account as a walk through the stories the city itself has to tell. He stands on the speaker's platform, surveys the forum, and lets forth a fiery discourse in which he cites the laws, recalls municipal decrees, appeals to the moral values the gods protect, refers to the sacrifices forefathers have made, and uses the glorious victories of the Empire as examples.

I've made this art my own. I am taking you on a tour of the city through the places in my memory as I stand here before you and speak. The words I pronounce are the words I mean to pronounce, they are measured, hewn, and riveted in the walls and monuments of the city. The events that these words describe are the events I remember. This memory is infallible, and these events are the events that took place, because they, just like my testimonial, are anchored in the route that I set down; they are woven with the stories this city has to tell. Your objection that this city doesn't have an agora or a forum, and that municipal decrees and laws are no longer set in stone, is irrelevant. Our city bellows with meanings for whomever wants to listen. The monument to the admirals of the Battle of Tolo on 1818 Square relates how dilapidated schooners, rowed with courage, willpower, and cunning, helped an imposing flotilla to the depths. At the Flower Market, just on the corner, there's a mounted statue of Randolfus the Reckless, who died during the siege of 1457 when he rushed to assist his imperiled hoards by jumping off the city walls equipped with giant cloth wings. The doorway of the Belaus church on the square depicts the story of Thomas the Unbeliever. The restaurant directly opposite is called The Liar's Palace. The neighboring library of the Theological faculty is housed in a former girls' orphanage, that was founded by Margaretha van Abonk, who amassed a fortune by selling her body in high circles, fell prey to amnesia, and was visited in the Bishop of Alkala's bed by a vision of the Holy Virgin revealing her unsoiled womb. Upon which she was cured, remembered everything about her sinful life, repented, and began acting as a benefactress, leaving much behind to the city—including the brewery behind the Rivelath, which in the time of sexual depravity, plague, and polluted water saved the lives of many clergymen, citizens, and fallen women. Members of the jury, do I need to conjure up anything else?

And we don't need to limit ourselves to the annals of the city, which are blown along in the wind like an unbound manuscript to flutter down upon various public buildings and monuments. My own history is written in the facades too. I know this city. All my life I've loved her, lost her, longed for her, and lived in her. My city is my secret diary. Its chapters are inscrutable where jealous mistresses are concerned and spread around several locations for safety. But I reread the jottings of my past whenever I see a path, poplar, or post office where my past has played out. When I walk, as I walked on the April 13th in question, I leaf through the journal of my life and read, in episodic and achronological chapters, my own story which, just like this account, follows the lines of the city map. I will give you an example.

3/ We turned on to a side street off of Avenue Concordia, two grams of tobacco and two papers lighter after encountering that unusually-dressed tourist; it is called Gregory Street and leads to Fredo Square. I strolled along the sidewalk on the left, along the northern side of the street, because that's where the sun was shining and because the promising spring weather had disappointed. It was cold in the shade. The first building I passed on the corner of the Avenue Corcordia was a hotel. The name escapes me, but it is something like City Hotel or Center Hotel, or Hotel Centrum, in any case a name that befits a hotel in the center of the city. This is where one late and drunken night Mira and I, in a virtuoso performance, pretended to be a Polish tourist and his pregnant spouse for the night porter. We had what had seemed to us a well-conceived plan, which was to give false names and vanish without a trace in the morning. We were as horny as young rats, at least I was, and few things are as exciting as expensive hotel rooms. You're anonymous and in a strange place. There are unfamiliar noises in the corridor, in the rooms next to you and above you, and out on the street. You feel like you've gone to a big party in a strange house full of strangers and you've hooked up with the half-drunken girlfriend of someone whose name you don't know in somebody else's bedroom. You can lock the door, but you never know who else might have a key. Everything in the room is designed for sex. The space is dominated by a large, unfamiliar, soft bed that smells of other women. The deep-pile carpet acts as an extension of the bed. The mirrors show a view of the bed. The remaining furniture disappears into the background and functions primarily as a depository for torn-off clothing. The window with its open curtains transforms your bed, high up over a strange street, into a peepshow. And unseen eyes bore into every pore of your back. Every cell in your body feels that this bed was occupied just last night by a bank manager and his blonde secretary, her tantalizing silk blouse hovering above legs so long that they cause you to weep with despair. And the night before that by a porn-film director and two delectable starlets, who know they have to agree to everything and arch their backs photogenically with feigned lust. You can hear unimaginable fantasies being played out in every neighboring room. In a hotel you can cheat with your own lover: even your own wife smells like an illicit mistress there. And you know that the maid who will come in the next morning without knocking is from Costa Rica, or the Philippines, and she'll look at you with languid eyelashes and eyes that could smelt steel. And she knows that she's disturbing you, but she doesn't leave, and she looks at you for just a fraction too long. And she doesn't speak, and her bronze body is suggesting and hinting beneath her black skirt and white blouse, because under her uniform she's as outrageously naked as a woman. And she looks at you again with doe-eyes and she smiles as she looks. And she looks like an African Queen looks, with two leopards purring at her feet and a hundred and ten naked black slaves dying of exhaustion in her bed of a thousand lion hides. And she stalks the bed like a panther. And she sits down on the edge of the bed like the Field Marshall of a powerful army. And she looks at me, and she doesn't speak. And she looks at me and caresses my neck like a lioness caresses the neck of an antelope. And she says nothing, and she looks at my body, mummified under the duvet, and she says nothing, and she looks like a pharaoh whose kneeling, chained-up, lowly minions are paying him tribute. And she says nothing, and she looks and she caresses the duvet like a tigress who is tearing an impala to shreds, its jaws dripping with blood. And she says nothing, and she looks and she caresses the duvet and she caresses very accurately, oh how she caresses, and I close my eyes and know I'm lost.

The night porter falls for it. He believes our story. Mira wrote Złedo-bova Zsčibivilovsčkaja or something like that in the guest book, with completely convincing upside down roofs on the c's or s's and a crossed l or two. She got so swept up in her role that even her handwriting had something Eastern-blockish and tipsy about it. But when the pen was handed to me, a black shiny official hotel pen on a little chain of chrome balls, and when the night porter in his official hotel uniform with polished buttons and imposing tassels looked at me in the official black marble hotel lobby and, in his officially polite hotel-English and his deep, official hotel voice, asked me in turn if I'd care to officially note down my official name, please, thank you very much, I stiffened, thanks or no thanks to my state of excitement, and lost faith in our cunning, drunken courage, and in Poland. I muttered that I'd forgotten something, sorry, first get some money out, sorry, be right back and dragged the divinely supple and voluptuous Złedobova Zsčibivilovsčkaja outside by the arm. She: angry. "What are you up to!" Me: playing the role of Rupert the Rightly and Responsible in an unconvincing manner. "We weren't really going to go through with it, you live round the corner, it was a good joke like that, come, we'll go to yours." She: even angrier. Argument. Slept apart that night, as usual.

The building next to the City Center Hotel is a tall, grouchy, residential house. There's never any light or movement behind its pinched up, suspicious windows. I used to believe that small boys were basted, roasted, and eaten here. But now I know better. It's the secret headquarters of a powerful crime syndicate; it is untouchable thanks to an ingenious rule: all of its members are blind. Behind the blacked-out windows, in the deepest, darkest depths of the night, they commit dark deeds which the daylight can't touch. Shady business is their element; in that respect they're untouchable. And the bashful glasses which dampen the light in their eyes, and the way they falter helplessly behind their red and white sticks, renders them above all suspicion.

Number 65 houses the Mercurius bookshop. This small business is run by a dusty fanatic who mispronounces the name of the every writer. It is actually quite amazing how he manages to mangle even the simplest ones. But don't underestimate him. He has read everything, and he has a phenomenal memory. He's a man with a message, as he always says, only he doesn't say what the message is. What's more, he's a great authority on classic action hero comics; his specialty is Batman, who he calls Beetman. I've heard that famous auction houses in America regularly seek his advice on the authenticity of rare, old issues. Faking Batmans seems like a fairly lucrative business to be in. Next to that is the entrance to the Budokai Sports School, where I was once, very briefly, tutored in the basics of kendo and aikido. I only took a couple of lessons, but I didn't need any more than that. Those born to the Path see through the principles of every martial art and assimilate them into their soul without having to get bogged down in the details of the particular techniques. Eus's Tattoos is at number 61. He's a gigantic beefcake who has had a good go at himself. He attends to his victims practically in the window, so that every passerby can see how many grimaces and teeth clenches a butterfly on the shoulder blade costs. If watching other people be tortured is one of the most reprehensible forms of voyeurism, the public staging of courage is one of the most perverse forms of exhibitionism, I think.

After that, I walked past The Weapon of Wagaland. I don't have a story for this one, only that every time I go past I'm amazed that I've never been in there. It has to be one of the few pubs in this part of town. I've never been to Wagaland either, and I dare to state that under oath, although I'd like to add that I don't share any of the usual prejudices against Wagalanders. Or wait a minute, I think this is the pub where Karin Horvath met the infamous Habold Sicx. Wagaland, that must be it. I remember that bastard Benno telling me the story, and I instantly thought: Wagaland, that's the pub whose hoary, unshaven farm dog of a reading table, upon which you could skin a live pig, pays homage to the place. Karin wrote a poem about hands that was so outrageously bad it has stayed with me always:

> All the things hands can make
> All the things hands can take
> All the things hands can say
> You can't take hands away.

She sent it off too, and to the most prestigious periodical there is, the cheeky bitch. Of course they didn't publish it. But Habold Sicx, one of the editors, the Publisher at the important press that has its offices around here, was so astonished by the lame quality of her submission that he wrote her a bold letter inviting her to have a drink with him. He wanted to know what kind of a girl was brave enough to submit such an exceptionally bad poem for publication in *Basanos*. They walked out of The Weapon of Wagaland hand in hand, their hair and thoughts both rumpled, and six months later they were married. Karin Horvath has since published a play and a novella—*The Pig Strangler*—about a young woman who breaks free from her provincial, farming background due to her courage and will-power. It's a bad book. I haven't read it. It sold really well and the reviews were alright, but everyone knows that's got less to do with her literary skills than the influence of her literary husband.

After that, I went past Sexyland without going in. As you know, that's where, for a modest fee, you can get a look at a naked girl for five minutes. You go down a steep, dark staircase, then you're in the basement, where it's warm and damp and the deforming acoustics transform hard dance music into hellish, other-worldly sounds. The dirty manager, always wearing the same gray jumper, sits there at his desk. He stinks. You pay him. Yet again he tries to con a double fee out of you, despite the fact that he recognizes you. Yet again he gets instant gratification when you pay half the amount he has asked for. Next he points you towards one of the five dark cubbyholes which can be closed from outside with a rickety bolt. The floor is sticky. Once you're inside, he presses a button behind his desk and a little slot about the size of a letterbox opens. If the slot doesn't open, he, whose only daily task is to press the right one of five buttons when he has customers, has pressed the wrong one. Shouting is pointless in all that noise, you have to come out of your hutch and tell the man he's made a mistake. He wants you to pay again. When you refuse, he points you towards the hutch that corresponds to the button he's wrongly pressed. You've already lost one and a half minutes of your five. The opened letterbox reveals a dimly lit room in which there's a bed. You have to be quite supple to be able to see the bed, especially when you're as tall as I am, because the architect has worked on an average eye height of 150 cm. So you have to spread your legs wide and bend over—this is not the most ideal position for masturbation. You have to push your buttocks hard against the door of the cramped hutch too, and the rickety bolt is not usually intended for that. A naked girl lies on the dimly lit bed. She tries to win your love by touching herself. She kneads her big, saggy breasts and pulls her labia open. Sometimes she's considerate enough to push one or two fingers inside. She does her best to look really sultry while doing it. She regularly makes licking motions with her tongue—this means that she really wants you. When the manager decides that your five minutes are up he presses the button again, which he clearly hadn't mistaken in the first place, and the slot snaps shut. If the mutual love has grown so great in the interim that you can't bear to say farewell to your bride just yet, you can persuade the manager to grant you five more minutes of her company for the right fee. Yes, members of the jury, denial is pointless, Rupert has visited Sexyland's indecent basement, and more than once. And I might as well admit everything to you at once: if that embarrassing incident, due to which I no longer dare go there, had never taken place, on Sunday, April 13th, I would also undoubtedly have descended into the underworld of my desires.

The specialists and enthusiasts among you will be surprised that I have frequented that filthy basement. It's true, I know much better peepshows. Even back then I'd had the opportunity to compare my basement with the luxurious voyeurs' palaces of Amsterdam, London, and Paris. And you don't have to convince me that those low letterboxes and rickety bolts don't measure up to the smoothly zooming carousels—which are tastefully lit and surrounded by comfortable private cabins with conservatory-style windows offering a clear, unencumbered view of nature's beauty. Even this city has dozens of establishments that offer more quality and service than that dirty basement and its five-buttoned dog. I must counter your suspicion that my preference for this location might have been coupled with a preference for a particular naked girl. While some naked girls are more beautiful and more naked than others, I've never walked down that dark, steep staircase out of a longing for my Eurydice. No, members of the jury, it wasn't romanticism that drove Rupert there. On the contrary. It was the dark, steep staircase—a secret, forbidden wormhole in the day, in the street, and in the world. A staircase to an underbelly teeming with lust, from whence it's quite possible you'll never return. It was that warm, damp basement, you felt dirty and sticky and able to do anything. It was that thumping, stamping organ music, fit for a pagan Mass, which took away your ability to think. It was that growling Cerberus, always present behind you like a threat. It was that cramped, dirty cubbyhole, a confessional box for the most bizarre sins. It was that sticky floor, a whore who allowed hundreds to ejaculate onto her. It was that rickety bolt which could jump from its slot at any moment, exposing your lowliest desires to the world. It was the whole ambiance. It was a mnemonic site for horniness which spread like a weed and sowed horniness in me whenever I passed that place on my wanderings. What drove me there, members of the jury, was filthy obscenity, capitulation to forbidden fantasies, and the consciousness of danger. That was the rotting layer of humus from which the stink-ball of my lust would surface, grow, and burst. I'm not proud of it, and I would have kept quiet if it wasn't of capital importance to the full understanding of my case, and if it might have formed the motive for the deed against which I defend myself today.

I realize that I'll have to pay for bringing in Sexyland as exonerating evidence by giving you the necessary explanation as to why, on the April 13th in question, I didn't visit the place, and why I hadn't dared to show myself there in the months before that either. This is not a story I'm happy to tell. I've never told it to anybody, and I would give a lot right now to spare myself the embarrassment of recounting the painful incident. But I won't withhold the facts from you. I trust that you will see my attention to these matters as proof of my respect for you and the rectitude you embody. But I also hope you will show some understanding if I limit my description of the event to the bare essentials.

On that fateful afternoon, the naked girl on duty was particularly gifted. Not that she was beautiful, on the contrary, she was exciting in a vulgar, dirty way. I stood wide-legged and bent forwards, raped her with my eyes, and let myself go. I have to admit to having pulled my pants down for a better grip. That wasn't anything unusual in itself. What was unusual was that it went on for five minutes longer than normal. That was why, along with her being so good at her job, my excitement became excruciating, and there was no alternative but to relieve myself. When I was right at the point of bursting, someone tugged on the door from the outside. The rickety bolt gave no resistance. It was the filthy manager, whom I'd never seen leave his desk before. After five minutes he'd pressed the switch, the right one, as always, and had correctly concluded that something had gone wrong with the automated closing mechanism when I didn't come out. I straightened up and turned around in shock. I saw myself in his eyes. There I was, Rub-off Rupert, my pants around my ankles, eye to eye with the stinking King of the Underworld, and I couldn't hold it in any longer. Worse still, the realization I'd been caught jolted through my underbelly like an electric shock and made the hellish agony worse than ever. Great dollops shot into the air and were thrown in a parabolic arch over his gray sweater, his gray pants, and his gray shoes. In some ways, it was the best sex I've ever had. But you will understand that such an experience doesn't lend itself to repetition and that, following my overhasty flight, I have never dared to return to the warm, damp chasms that were once so beloved to me.

The house on the right of Sexyland is where Giannis once lived, a guy I met in the pub. He was a perfect drinking partner with a motto: Never do anything because doing something always makes it worse. There was a time when I spoke to him practically on a daily basis. He invited me to his house on several occasions, but I never went. I haven't seen him for years. I've lost his new address.

The first floor of the building next to that, 53A Gregory Street, was for sale at a time when I could have afforded to buy an apartment. I viewed it with an estate agent from Hestia Properties; she was just like you've always wanted estate agents to be but how they never are: tall and blonde, suited and booted, with her hair in an up-do. She was in excellent condition, nicely done up, well-maintained on the outside and with several authentic features. She was ready to move into. And the most beautiful thing about her was her nervousness. She wanted to move further up the ladder in Hestia Properties, but she was not quite clever enough and a little too stupid to realize that. She was paid on commission and it hadn't worked out too well recently. Her colleagues had been making jokes about her behind her back. She had to sell this house, at all costs. And as Rupert happened to be the one traipsing through the bedrooms with her, Rupert, for the love of god, had to be seduced into a transaction. She tried to hide it behind a mask of routine, foundation, and professionalism, but I felt how the need to succeed at all costs raced through her loins like a forest fire getting out of control. It left her prepared to do anything. "The fuse box is in good order. But I'm actually more interested in your fuses. Two groups, right?" I could have given the word and she would have hurried to service me, with excuses for her negligence. Equally, I could have said nothing and pushed her gently onto the current owner's bed. She wouldn't have put up any resistance. She would have catered to her customer's requirements with a professional touch. But Rupert is not like that. I'm a stranger to such thoughts. However much she would have liked to unbutton herself then and there in the semi open-plan kitchen with built in appliances, and give me a good view of the upstairs, I acted nobly and didn't give her the slightest encouragement to compromise herself. The apartment was amazing by the way. The neighborhood was also really to my tastes. But I didn't dare to telephone her with an offer and ask whether we might possibly meet up sometime for a quick drink if she felt like it too. When I walked past it again two weeks later the house had been sold. I didn't go and visit the other apartments in the building. They couldn't have lived up to the dream of 53A Gregory Street.

There's a hairdresser's at Number 51. It used to be called Ladies and Gentlemen's Hair Salon and it looked like a ladies and gentlemen's hair salon, but, because reality can't be as well marketed as a concept of reality, it's now called Hair Philosophy and looks like a trendy coffee bar for New York intellectuals, with an aluminum reading table and sophisticated halogen lighting. To underpin the philosophical angle of their image-building, they've added a few bookcases with real books, and the window displays a line that actually comes from a real poem but still sounds hip:

MIXING MEMORY AND DESIRE

Sometimes when I walk by, I allow myself ever wilder imaginings about a Wasteland Cut, but that's just another example of typical European arrogance towards New York intellectuals, of course.

After that, I turned left through the entranceway to an idyllic alley in which, if you listen carefully, you can still hear the rattling of coach wheels on the cobbles. This small street has the improbable name of Alley of a Thousand Sighs, but, in the ever jocular vernacular which never misses a trick, it's called the Alley of a Thousand Thighs. She lived there at Number 15, on the second floor. I've known her in every corner of the city and I lost her in Manora Street, but here, in this inconveniently arranged studio apartment, with its heavy, dark beamed ceiling, is where I made a conquest of Mira. Ladies and gentlemen of the jury, we're coming to the crux of my case.

4 / She was my martyrdom, my masochism, and my sugar-sweet, shimmering Mira. She appeared like a reflection before my eyes the first time I saw her, she killed me when she was mine, and she finally brought me back to life when she'd murdered me for good. She was the Spring sun that lured me outside with its radiance and the city in which I lost myself. I dreamed of her warm, messy sluggishness when she didn't want to get up in the morning, her ravishing, impromptu presence in the afternoon, her conversations between mirrors in her sparklingly-decorated favorite local, and her deadly seductions after sunset. She was like the three Muses, as gloriously lifelike as the most beautiful goddesses in a mystical painting that had been completed by an angel in a dream, and she was like the lady of seven times seven roses who stole the actor's roles. She was all the women that I had ever imagined and worshipped a thousand times; she was seven times seven more beautiful than them, and she was real. She was the fact that makes fiction impossible. And in all her unparalleled reality she belittled me only to erect me once she'd broken me for good and reduced me to a dream.

I met her by chance; how else could it have happened? Benno, the bastard, had taken me with him to a party of a college friend we had in common. We hadn't seen him for ages because he'd left the city. The party was a long way away, all the way over in Kse-Waga in Wagaland, and before I'd even climbed on board the hydrofoil I was regretting letting him convince me to join him. But to turn back would be an insult to our crazy plan just to go; it would be a nice trip anyway, mustn't grumble, would be a shame to stay home. The party was disappointing. There was homemade punch, lots of wine, peanuts, and people, but hardly anyone we knew. I wanted to go home early, but as usual I was lacking the will power to decide not to stay, and before I knew it, it was so late there was no reason not to stay later. So I wavered back and forth between nuts and bottles, openers and ashtrays, room and garden, garden and toilet, toilet and room, conversations and chats, and reminiscences with the former college friend, to whom I actually had little to tell. Benno, the bastard, had already gone home. I had just poured yet another last glass, gone back out to the garden, where I'd slowly rolled another excellent cigarette, and was standing for a while smoking on my own, casually, without any deep thoughts, plan, or having passed judgment about anything whatsoever, when suddenly there she was. She hit me like a bullet in the head. She was lovely, and more than that—she was real. I was so stunned I couldn't think of anything else to do but ask her if she needed a light perhaps. "That's very sweet of you, thanks, but I don't smoke." I didn't know what else to say then. "But do give me a light if you want to. Then I'll act all sultry and we can look into each other's eyes. That's what you want isn't it?" I laughed heartily, as if I was casually laughing at a good joke, but she had dark green eyes that shone like the eyes of a predator in the jungle, and I knew that I could never let her go. "Give me a bit of your wine. My glass is empty. What's your name, then?" Rupert the Irrational introduced himself and didn't know how to carry on with his life. Although I was in no state to ask the obvious question, she told me that she was called Mira. When she asked where I was from, the wonderfully, heavenly, oh what luck, happened. It turned out that she had studied in Kse-Waga but had had problems with one or other of her teachers. She'd decided to move to our city. She had just, two days previously, found a single-roomed apartment with a beautiful, old beamed ceiling, on the second floor in a street with a crazy name in the heart of the city. She'd be moving in later that week. "I have to go, Rupert. It was really nice meeting you here. Now at least I know one person in the city. Shall we arrange to meet? Would you like to come and see my new apartment? I'd really like that. What about next weekend? Saturday night? I'll cook for you. It will be great to cook something nice in my new home in my new city for my new friend." Rupert could make next weekend Saturday night. Oh boy could Rupert make it. She kissed me three times in the usual manner. "Bye. I really have to go now. But I'll see you next week. You will come, won't you?" Rupert was left in that dark garden, and he was like a remote island in the ocean over which a devastating hurricane had just blown. Yes, certainly, Rupert would come. Of course he'd come. He couldn't wait until Saturday.

5/The St. Pierre filets she'd cooked were disappointing. Not that I was hungry. It was going well, it wasn't going badly, it mustn't go wrong, it had to work. There were almost no silences. She'd drunk a lot of wine too. She'd laughed at a few jokes. Desert was tiramisu. There was a relaxed atmosphere, it had to be relaxed at all costs. I did my utter best to act normal. More wine, and she drank more wine too. The wine was good. It wasn't going badly, it mustn't go badly. She seemed to be relaxing, she had to relax at all costs. More jokes, because she laughed at my jokes. I was on form, I had to be on form, I had to show my best side, I had to be Rupert the Interesting and Rupert the Charming and Rupert the Irresistible Knight, her dream lover, the name of her thousand sighs.

"A little bit more wine?"

"Yes please, lovely. Fill my glass. It's lovely wine."

It went well. Everything went according to the book. The conversation was relaxed, but was actually *about* something. I was a man of depth, I had to be a man of depth, with whom you could discuss life's big questions, but I didn't have to be, because I wasn't a snob who couldn't make small talk. I mustn't be a snob. But it went well, it didn't go badly, it mustn't go badly. The table looked antique but wasn't. That was good. We sat at one corner of the table. That was good. I had to try to shunt my chair a bit closer to her. There was wine. The wine was good. More wine. We must drink a lot of wine. She'd put out candles. That had to mean something. She drank more wine than she must have intended. That had to mean something too. The signals were clear. It was going well. I'd made jokes and she'd laughed. She'd put some good music on. How beautiful she was. Rupert, she is your woman. Don't let her go. Tonight you must make her yours. Can you please not disappoint me for once, Rupert. Not this time. This time not. You can do it. Tonight. I implore you.

"A little bit more tiramisu?"

"Yes, please, lovely. You're a really good tiramisu cook."

It went well. I was charming and elegant. I was wearing my loose, white shirt over my button-up jeans. I was wearing the belt with the cool, big buckle. I was Rupert Dean, the irresistible tragic hero of every girl's bedroom. I looked good, well-shaven but not too smooth. It was also good that I hadn't ironed my shirt. I was a free-living lad who wasn't bothered about that sort of superficiality. She was getting more beautiful by the minute. It was going well, it mustn't go wrong. I had to watch out that I wasn't too vulgar, but it went well. I maintained a sunny disposition, but every now and then I allowed an almost imperceptible black cloud to blow across my face, suggesting that I was withholding a dark secret that I might tell her.

"Would you like another glass?"

"Well, I do have a glass here, but perhaps something to go in it?"

She laughed. It was going well. I was funny and straight forward. I shunted my stool unnoticed, just a few more millimeters in her direction. The wine hung like a mist in the room. Do something, it's time to do something, high time, it's now or never, she'll be like putty in your hands, the signals are there and more, it is clear and proven, it's actually always been clear, don't be afraid, she's waiting for you to do something, be cool, be brave, look at her, be a hero for once, Rupert the Virgin-Slayer, strike with the ease of a romantic hero, no delay will be tolerated, strike while the iron's hot, the wine hangs like mist in the room and is making her lose her inhibitions, she is just a bit shy, the dear sweet thing, but what she'd love you to do, your darling, is to do something, dear Rupert, her love, do something for love, now's the time, look at her, say something in a deep voice, do something with a steady hand, do something, Rupert, now.

"Shall we open another bottle?"

"Why not? A bird never flew on two wings. It's nice here with you. I do fancy another glass," I said in a deep voice. You have to say her name, say her name, that'll soften her. "Mira, you know what, Mira, it's so nice here talking with you, that we can talk so easily to each other. It's as if we've known each other for years. Don't you think, Mira?" I sang the last Mira in a deep contrabass, like a Russian orthodox priest chanting in the dark night in the somber everglades of the Volga. Immediately, I fell into a coughing fit.

"Here. Take a big sip. Have you got a cold? Your voice sounds a little odd as well."

"Thanks. No, it's nothing. I'm choking." Oh, she was beautiful.

6 The art of seduction is one of the most intensively studied aspects of the art of being human. Much thought has been given to it over the course of centuries; it has been researched more, and written about more, than any other discipline, which might seem surprising, given that the premise is always the same: man wants woman. But despite the astonishing simplicity of the problem, the number of methods and techniques which have been suggested to achieve man's desire are endless and innumerable. Man grabs woman by the hair, throws her into his cave, clubs her senseless, and takes her. Man practices the art of poetry and lyre-playing his whole life, composes an ode to a woman, and, on a balmy summer's night, in the moonlight and the scent of roses, serenades her under her balcony. Man goes to a disco, pinches a woman's backside, and shouts in her ear, "Would you like to go outside and look at the motorcycles?" Man has himself raised up in his suit of armor and in that armor onto a horse, then gallops past a woman and pierces other suits of armor with his lance. Man buys flowers for a woman and has them delivered to her house accompanied by a card. Man conceals himself in the night behind a tree in the park and when a woman cycles by, shows her his erection. Man goes to study economics at Yale or Princeton, lands a well-paid job, buys a red Ferrari, and displays his keys conspicuously on the table when he dines with a woman. Man plays guitar, takes drugs, and, sweating on a podium, croons songs of love and loss (in English) in a lived-in voice. Man goes to father of woman and buys her. Man becomes helpless and employs a woman to nurse him. Man bumps a woman with his car, gently, when she's on a crosswalk and takes her to the hospital, just as a precaution. Men calls a woman on the phone and asks her if she'd like to go for a drink with him. Man is crowned sultan and orders woman to join his harem. Man takes woman out for a drink and drops Spanish fly in her Coca-Cola when she's in the bathroom. Man spends his last dime on a Greyhound ticket to Hollywood, makes sure he's discovered, acts in romantic films, wins an Oscar, comes across a woman at a party on the producer's estate, and says hello. Man follows a woman when she's walking home at night, pushes her into a dark stairway, and holds a knife to her throat. And this is only a tiny fraction of the possibilities and methods represented in the literature on the subject.

In the light of these innumerable studies, it is astonishing that that the crucial aspect of the art of seduction remains completely undiscussed. In the end, everything comes down to bridging a gap of forty centimeters. There I sat, Rupert the Conqueror, at Mira's mock antique dining table in an awkwardly arranged room, Mira's room, with a heavy, dark-beamed ceiling, Mira's ceiling. We sat at a corner of the table and Rupert wanted Mira. Everything had progressed according to the book. She had cooked filets de St. Pierre which had been disappointing, but I wasn't hungry. There had been wine, lots of wine, and candlelight. The right music had played on her cheap stereo. Everything had gone well, the atmosphere was relaxed, I had cracked a few jokes, and she had laughed. She had become more beautiful by the minute. I had been charming and elegant, my outfit tossed together with just the right degree of nonchalance, clean-shaven but not too smooth, pleasant company but also hinting at a dark secret which I'd never, ever told anyone. I had said her name in a deep voice. We had drunk more wine than she had intended and the time had slipped by unnoticed. And all the while I had inched my chair, little by little, centimeter by centimeter to the left, toward the table leg which separated my left leg from her right one. I had placed my left arm, naturally, on my left knee, and I reached out under the table until I was almost doubled over in order to accidentally brush against her right knee, but it hadn't worked out. And so there I sat and everything had gone well and she sat on my left and the space between us was no more than forty centimeters. Forty centimeters separated my hand from her neck and my mouth from her drunken, wine-flavored lips. Forty centimeters was the breadth of the Grand Canyon, the Atlantic crossing, the distance from Earth to Mars. I had come within forty centimeters of happiness, and I didn't know how I was going to bridge this gap.

But it was better this way. It was definitely much better. I would drink one more glass of wine, calmly and with dignity, then I would stand up, proffer elegant words of thanks for the generous dinner and her most charming company, and then, with head held high and pride intact, I would wander, calmly and with dignity, through the dead town to my own home and bed. Undoubtedly, other men had sat at her table before me, on this chair, and had feasted their itchy paws on her goddess-like body before the main course. But Rupert is no such man. I am a stranger to such thoughts. Even though she wouldn't have liked anything more than to let herself be seduced on the spot, right on her mock antique dining table, I displayed my nobility and gave her no opportunity to compromise herself. It would be a relief to her, a marvel that would lead her to repent. That same night, alone in her bed, she would think of me in admiration, the same way that a young prostitute in Palestine lay in bed at night remembering the Messiah she had seen walk by that morning. She would conclude that not all men are the same. Rupert was different. There were still noble and honorable knights in this world. She would not fall in love with me, but it would dawn on her for the first and last time that true love did exist. She would no longer be able to get me out of her mind, day and night she'd think of me, until she plucked up the courage to call me and to ask me over again. And then she would inch her chair, little by little, centimeter by centimeter, toward the table leg which separated her right leg from my left one. She would lay her right arm awkwardly on her right leg and stretch under the table until she was almost doubled over in order to accidentally brush against my right leg. She would tremble with longing and love. The roles would be reversed, and her whole body would sigh with happiness when I stood up at the end of the evening and finally, at long last, took her in my arms with a simple and powerful gesture and kissed her.

"And now action," she said, "Enough beating about the bush. Is something going to come of this, brave knight? Come and give me a nice kiss. I feel like going to bed with you."

7 Fade out. Black screen. Next scene: morning. Setting: bedroom. Fiery, warm golden sunlight plays through the curtains and colors the screen with happiness. Piles of random clothing are scattered around the floor. Camera zooms in on a dream of a bed with clean, white satin sheets. Bed in suggestive disarray. In bed, to the right of the audience, lies Rupert, asleep on his back. The clean, white satin sheets don't quite manage to cover all of his smooth, athletic torso. Also visible: part of his left hip and a beautifully muscled dream of a left leg, not overly hairy. Left in bed—Mira, asleep on her left side. Her happily-dreaming head rests on Rupert's right shoulder; her right arm, naturally and tenderly, but also suggestively, on top of the clean, white satin sheets, under which lies Rupert's lower body. Smile on her sleeping face. Ray of sunlight caresses her right breast. Rupert awakes. Opens eyes, turns head slowly to the right. Looks at sleeping Mira with an expression that shows the following feelings: happiness, recognition of his life-long sought other half, deep fulfillment, tenderness, and true love. Rupert very carefully kisses Mira on her warm, sleeping mouth. Mira kisses back in her sleep and then opens her eyes. Looks at Rupert with a smile which means the following: she has awoken into a dream, Rupert is a god, and the world is good. Mira strokes Rupert's left cheek with the back of her right hand. Camera zooms in further on both of them looking at each other. No dialogue. The dreamy gazes alone are enough to show that no two people in the world have ever loved each other as much as Rupert and Mira. The end.

Audience remains sitting in darkened room for minutes on end with a lump in their throats and damp eyes as the credits roll.

Ladies and gentlemen of the jury, if I were a free man and master of my destiny instead of your defendant, and if I were allowed to sketch out the scenario that my longings had deserved instead of the faithful account of the facts that I must explain to you without roses, perfume, or gold-leaf, I would have left that dark night to your romantic imagination and would have ended here, on that evening, with that happy dream and with this happy end, because that's how she was, you could never turn the page on her. How can I describe her? Like God, she can only be defined by what she isn't. She wasn't like Cynthia, who still lived at home, kissed like a vacuum pump, and gave me a hand job in the alleyway next to her parent's back garden. Nor was she like Delia, who wasn't really my type and was actually quite fat, but who, despite her girth, had lost her virginity when she was twelve to a boy with a car, who'd experienced her first threesome when she was sixteen, and there were photos of that, and who allowed me to use her like an inflatable doll. Nor was she like Clodia, little Clodia who only dared to do it in the dark, which I didn't mind since she looked too sweet to be sexy. Nor was she like Corinna, who looked like Cynthia. Nor was she like Neaira, who poked her tongue into the corner of her mouth, whispered the things they whisper in films, and wanted me to come on her breasts because that's how she thought you were supposed to do it. Mira was everything they weren't. She was the fantasy I'd kissed, stroked, and adored in all my previous girlfriends without knowing that she was it. And she wasn't that fantasy because she breathed as a woman, smelled like a woman, and felt like a woman. She was the dream I'd spent years dreaming next to other women, but she wasn't a dream, she was made of female flesh, creamy like the paper of an expensive edition of the most desperate *Dolce Stil Novo* love lyrics from the Duecento. And I leafed through her blouse and sniffed the aroma of longing on her marbled end papers—they rippled with promise. She unbuttoned the hooks on her back and showed me the title page, which was a wonder of graphic design, symmetry, and pure poetry. I stroked her breasts as if I were carefully fingering an engraving of the Judgment of Paris; the anonymous master had surpassed himself: you could almost feel the curves, they seemed to mound up out of the paper like real breasts.

Because an angel had guided his hand and an angel guided my hand over her breasts, and I wished I had two golden apples to give to her. "Do you like them? They're all yours." I coughed up an answer through the mountain of rice pudding I had been obligated to eat in order to gain entry to the Land of Milk and Honey, where sweet, black wine rains down onto your drunken lips each day. She smiled, and her smile was a story you could lose yourself in. And she pushed my head away. She took the book out of my hands to have me read an even better poem. She pointed to where it was. She unbuttoned her jeans, undid the zip, opened up the pages, and pushed the verses under my nose. I read like I was falling from the world, and I read a poem that smelled of the warm pelts of animals sacrificed to Artemis and that sang of a longing that was a sea to drown in; the pain of completeness, death, and love; and of mortals nourished with the bread of dreams, and who are singed by the blinding beauty of an angel. I read the poem and my tongue hung out in amazement as I followed the lines. Oh, how I followed those lines and how I tasted every verse; they expressed, for the first time, what I had always known. I read myself and lost myself forever in that poem. She smiled, and her smile was a sea to drown in. And she pushed my head away. She took the book from my hands to show me myself. And she stood before the smelting looks of my longing, naked, and as tangible as Pygmalion's statue become flesh and blood, and she was complete, the epiphany of a goddess thousands of artists have venerated in their work and whose representations have always fallen unutterably short— how could they know? Mira, my Mira, she was my dream incarnate.

"You hadn't expected that, had you, that you'd be able to seduce me tonight? You look at me like you find me beautiful. You mustn't underestimate yourself, Rupert, you are an Irresistible Virgin-Slayer. I'd put money on the fact that you could have any woman, but they should keep their dirty hands off you because I want you to be mine. Come here. Just mine. Don't look at me like that, you're making me shy. Come here. You're too hot in all these clothes. I want you, Rupert. I've wanted you all night. I wanted you from the moment I first saw you. What a lot of buttons. Do these cuffs need unbuttoning? And I know that you want me a little bit too. I'll be good for you. So, glasses off, you don't need those any more, I'll be right next to you. Lift up your arms. There, that's better.

You didn't want to keep these lovely shoulders from me, did you? What an egotist, not wanting to let me see your bare chest. You're a real man, Rupert. A real, tough man of a man. With a cool belt with a big, strong buckle. Can I see how it opens? Nice buckle, it opens really easily. You're a man of the world, I can see that from your buckle. And a button-up fly, well, well, that too. Come, don't be shy. I want you. You won't disappoint me. Shoes off. Pants off. Hurry up. I want to see all of you. I want to see the lovely man who has so powerfully seduced me. I feel like loving you the whole night long until we collapse in exhaustion. Red tulips, how sweet. You've put on your nicest boxer shorts just for me, with your delicious buttocks to grab. And it's much nicer to grab them in real life, without the flowers. I love you, Rupert. I want to see the naked reality. Let me check if you're a boy. You can wear those nice boxers again tomorrow. Yes, you're a boy. Scientifically proven. A shy, little boy. How sweet. Don't be so shy, Rupert. There's no need for that. Relax. I'll indulge you, adore you, love you, and everything in between. Come next to me on the bed. Come, Rupert."

And Rupert got onto the bed, drunk and dizzy from being in love and from Mira's body. She kissed, stroked, bit, whispered, and licked. It wasn't her fault. She adored me like a goddess. And I did my utter best. I tried to think about everything I always think about, but I smelled, tasted, felt, heard, and saw the real Mira. I thought about Shyla Foxx in a gym with six instructors between her volcanic tits, but the entire photo series was dimmed by the pearly marble of her sculpted breasts. I thought about the lap dancer from The Pole Bar who, for a ten euro note, had whispered fantasies in my ear that had kept me busy for a month, but she whispered in my ear that she loved me. I thought about the tall blonde girl I'd seen walking along the street, who'd deliberately ignored me in order to seduce me, but she worshipped every part of my body with her caresses. I thought about Cynthia who'd jerked me off in the darkness like a milking machine, but she was radiant, soft, and lovely. I thought about Corinna, who looked like Cynthia, who I could fuck as if I was fucking Cynthia, but she was more real than the dream I'd dreamt with Cynthia. I thought about three fingers in a worn-out cunt that I'd spied through a peep hole that was 150 cm above the floor, but before me I saw the gleaming pelt of an unusually beauteous and intelligent animal.

I thought about Jenna Jameson, with her heartbreaking hungry look and a heartbreaker tattoo on her right buttock, playing an estate agent in the film *Total Surrender* and going to strange houses and offering herself to potential buyers of either sex, and I offered myself entirely to her, but she looked at me with loving eyes. I thought about Neaira, copying Jenna Jameson because that's what she thought you were supposed to do, but she was unique and outrageously amazingly herself. I thought about the photos Delia had shown me of herself lying there doubly filled, but she was passion, she was alive, and she lived for me. I thought about women with horses, but she kissed me as if I were a man. I thought about the stinking Cerberus from Sexyland who growled threateningly behind Mira's bedroom door, but she embraced me and I knew I was safe. I even thought about Clodia, little Clodia, who hardly dared, but she kissed me and her eyes told me that all was well and that all would be well forever. But it was not well. She was my longing become flesh, but my longing refused to become flesh.

"It doesn't matter," she said. "You're sweet."

"It's the wine," I said. But it wasn't the wine.

8 This is the certifiable truth, the record of my first night with Mira, enjoyed in an idyllic alleyway with an improbable name, on the second floor of Number 15. It is said that every beginning is difficult. An experienced crocodile hunter once explained that the very first crocodile is the hardest to catch. He therefore advises his students to always begin with the second. It is also said that true love must show its weaknesses, and that whoever shows his worst side on the first night will never be able to disappoint his wife again for the rest of her life. I wish they were right.

Gentlemen of the jury, it wasn't the wine. And each new crocodile was even more threatening, until finally I decided to avoid them altogether. To this day I haven't been able to work out what the problem was. Everything was working physically—in that sticky basement in Sexyland and elsewhere, as I have repeatedly and ardently proved. Mira was everything I'd ever dreamed of. In fact, she was my first and last love; she was sweet to me and her techniques were accomplished. The thing I wanted most in the whole world dammit was to love her normally, like I should, according to the book, just simply and thoughtlessly, like every bastard of a man can love his woman. But whenever we tried it again, with total conviction that every beginning is difficult and that it doesn't matter if the beginning goes on for longer than expected, I watched on powerlessly as my desires shrank. Who would have thought it, Rupert had become impotent. The joke of the century, I laughed myself silly. But Rupert wasn't impotent because everything worked perfectly. Just not with Mira. But it wasn't Mira's fault because she was my dream incarnate. It was a satanic riddle without a solution. If you fed it into a super-computer it would come back in a loop that would burn through all the circuitry. It was enough to drive you mad.

Of course, during the seven months that I was her impotent boyfriend, and in all the months since, I have repeatedly come up with hypotheses concerning the cause of my defect. I thought it might be due to the awkward set up of the room, with its dark-beamed ceiling. My theory was that this location had been transformed into a memory site for frustrated desires through that first traumatic night. According to that theory, Number 15, second floor apartment, Alley of a Thousand Sighs, was a sort of mirror universe of Sexyland. I only needed to descend the stairs into that warm, damp chasm and I had an erection before I'd even paid the doorman. In the same way, the stairs up to her room would cut me down before I'd even kissed her. This theory was plausible, but it turned out to be untenable. It didn't work at my house either, notwithstanding the fact that when she wasn't there this location did lend itself reasonably well to solitary excitements. There was no improvement when she moved to Manora Street either. At least not until that one afternoon which was the last. My second hypothesis was based on the revolutionary concept of the living topos. I came up with a theory that she herself had become a mnemonic site for my impotence. In a paradoxical way, the sight of her sensual body triggered my memory, recalling my inability to show her my love, just as whenever I saw Giannis I felt a hangoverish headache dawning. In its favor, I came to realize, during a process of careful self-analysis, that my thoughts have the tendency to reread themselves, which is something like my preference to repeatedly re-walk my habitual route through the city. Although I haven't been able to falsify this theory, it seems dangerous to accept it. It would be poor scientific method to base an explanation on the dubious observation of a breathing, scented, and kissing mnemonic site, the more so since there is no record of such a phenomenon in the literature.

Now that I have the advantage of being able to consider the history of my inability from some historic distance, I'm inclined to seek an explanation in the area of the appropriation of roles between actors and audience and the relationship between fact and fiction. I will try to clarify what I mean.

Imagine that there was once a great theatre actor called Rupert. Evening after evening he walked the planks, evening after evening he enjoyed great triumphs as the passionate hero of numerous romantic plays about love, performing to an amorphous, invisible breathing mass in the darkness. On stage he seduced princesses, vestal virgins, fallen women, countesses, nuns, seamstresses, empresses, housewives, and other men's wives. He took them in his arms with a simple, powerful gesture, and when he kissed them like a dormant volcano the audience sighed along with the lucky characters. But on one ill-fated evening, after his thousandth thundering performance, a bouquet of seven times seven roses was delivered to his dressing room, followed by the woman of his dreams. He wanted to adore her until deep in the night and start growing old with her the next day. She wanted the same, closed her eyes, and opened her lips to offer herself to him. But he couldn't take her in his arms with a simple, powerful gesture. Although there's nothing he would have wanted more, he couldn't kiss her. We might suppose that this was due to the great romantic actor Rupert not being able to play himself. This explanation is not completely wrong, but the whole truth turns out to be more complex. It was also to do with the dark, breathing, and sighing crowd that was his audience. He wasn't able to embody their dreams without them. The fourth wall was his mirror, and without a reflection he didn't exist. It is often stated that theatre is a form of exhibitionism, and we know that the exhibitionist can only exist thanks to his symbiotic relationship with the voyeur. But for the romantic actor Rupert, this symbiosis was so deep-rooted that the roles had merged together. The audience didn't so much look at him as identify with him and play along with him, and he saw himself through the eyes of the audience. He was the voyeur of his own exhibitionism. When he was the Count van Montrof, who disguised himself as a stable boy, pinched the King's daughter's bottom, and tore the smock from her body, he foamed with passion because he was spying on his own character himself from the darkness. When he was Kasnov the Cossack, undressing farmer's daughters with his saber, he roared with love because he identified with his own actions in the darkest lodges of his soul. He was the most powerful lover on earth when he empathized with the role he was playing, through his own audience. His affections were fictions he made real by identifying with the spectator watching the character he brought to life. But the lady with the seven times seven roses was no dream. She was the woman of his dreams, and she stood there before him in all her real, delectable tangibility—she was nothing but fact. He couldn't kiss her because she was real and really real. There was no fiction he could make real, no role to play through which he could merge with his own audience.

I'll happily accept a better theory. Although I sense that much of this hypothesis is sound, I don't entertain the illusion that I've convinced you. If I'm honest, I have to admit that right now I'm not entirely sure my theory is tenable. And neither is it for me to sit in your place in this room and offer an explanation for what happened. I tell and you judge. As I'm sure you know, there's an aesthetic theory which maintains that the value of a literary work is dependent on the extent to which the reader is challenged to fill in the gaps in the story. In the same manner, let it be proof of my sincerity that I lay down the facts before you as they are, without my story being distorted by a literary plan that gives these facts coherence.

Members of the jury, I apologize for the fact that I have tried your patience with my extended digression about an unbelievable woman you don't know and an unbelievable ailment that so ill befits the character standing here before you. I can imagine that for the last half hour you must have felt more like a meager audience listening with feigned benevolence to a writer reading from his latest novel—during which time it becomes painfully clear that the helpless protagonist is being tortured with all the fictive dreams and nightmares that the author hasn't dared to implicate himself in—than like claws of justice that this court called to give an independent and unbiased judgment based on a factual account of the events on the Sunday, April 13th, in question as set down in the charge. But I swear under oath that the story of Rupert and Mira hasn't got a single trace of romantic fiction in it. On the contrary, and to my deep regret, it is a true story, as true as I stand here before you; real like the city through which I wandered aimlessly that aforementioned Sunday, and real in the way Mira was a dream become reality. This story has given me pause for thought, just as I paused for thought opposite Number 15,

Avenue of a Thousand Sighs on the aforementioned April 13th. And although I'm properly conscious that the burden of evidence concerning its pertinence to my case fully rests upon myself, I assure you that my case would have forfeited some of its intelligibility if I hadn't taken this side street. After the adjournment, I'll resume my journey.

THE SECOND HEARING

1 / The sun, who had marched into the city with shining arrogance, began to feel a little ashamed of her lack of vigor. She cast her eyes down and tried to hide herself behind a veil of clouds, just as a defendant hides his guilt under a cozy duvet of feathery words, but it only half works. A kind of menace had built up in the air, like that weather when people say "funny weather, isn't it?" while persevering at having a nice time outdoors on such a lovely day, only they grow uneasy and they're not sure why.

I continued along the Alley of A Thousand Sighs, which curves slightly to the right and then changes its name by the Market Hall. Then I turned left. I walked through the central corridor of the market to the square in front of the Church of the Holy Heart, which on a day like that is always full of street artists. I paused for a while to let them entertain me. Two festively decked-out students were going at it exhaustingly with unicycles, torches, different colored hats, cleavers, buckets of water, brave members of the public, and a chainsaw. To be honest, I spent more time looking at a tall, blonde girl who was licking an ice cream cone. She stood there licking exactly as a tall, blonde girl should: with seasoned skill. She knew that she was pretty, and she stood there knowing that in the same way that people know objects fall downwards or that the sun sets in the West. It was a given that every man would want her, and it bored her some-what. Naturally, she wore jeans with dark brown cowboy boots. When she broke away from the ring of spectators and walked off towards the

Helibora Street, I followed her with my eyes because her swaying blue buttocks were made to be looked at, and she knew that, and they swayed off perfectly, like two Hollywood divas on the red carpet, smiling into the flashing cameras. Once she'd disappeared from sight, it was time for me to go on my way. I walked along Murdon Street with the Church of the Holy Heart on my right, towards the Gondoliers Jacket, and there I turned right through the archway to Fredo Square.

"Excuse me, sir." It was a female tramp of the most fallen variety, hopelessly attempting to give herself airs, like a duchess down on her luck, but the airs her formless, filthy jogging pants were giving off had the penetrating stink of sweat and virulent old woman's piss. She obviously had a bad cold, unless the clot of phlegm she coughed up was a sign of further disintegration. She was a woman made for insults, clearly the type with the nerve to shamelessly ask for a cigarette and then could you make it two. I spot that kind of thing instantly. She was the sort that wrongly judges me, due to my calm and worthy gait, to be a man who will apathetically give in to intrusiveness. She was in for a nasty surprise.

"Excuse me, sir. *Voici votre carte*. Drowned Phoenician seaman. Drowned, but not by water." She had fished a dirty, well-thumbed tarot card out of her jogging pants. That was all I needed. "Look, the dark green predators that were her eyes. *Regardez!*"

The art of the insult is a skill that few can master. Most people yell out a few vulgar and insulting names, adopt an angry look, and think that's the end of it. But, like every art, it requires highly specific skills and talents, and many people underestimate that. First of all, the most successful insult requires the creation of an unbridgeable distance. Raising your voice has the opposite effect in this respect. The most likely scenario is that the object of your insults will reciprocate using the same weapon, resulting in a face-off between two bellowing baboons in which both appear equally ludicrous. It's better and more humiliating when your opponent decides not to let himself be drawn into a volume contest and quietly leaves. Idiots are tempted to see this retreat as a victory, but the opposite is true. It's the superior retreat of the laurelled man of battle whose eye is turned to matters of greater importance than a skirmish with a gang of barbarians who challenge him with pathetic war-cries on a strategically unimportant hill. Consequently, it is better to opt for the deadly weapon of civilization. Consider the example of Ishida Mit-sunari, an unbeatable samurai from the Sengoku period, who dressed impeccably and spoke like a poet. His calm and worthy elegance, the kind you'd sooner associate with a prince of the Imperial Court than with a warrior who had won four hundred and thirty-one battles, made him deadlier than the destructive power of his swords. Once, when he was traveling through the woods in the Fukushima Prefecture, he came across three brigands who had robbed the beautiful young courtesan, Michiko, of the Takeda family. They'd beaten off her escort, dragged her by the hair from her sedan chair, and were busy attending to her in violent ways. Six randy hands had torn her silver silken kimono from her body, and her parchment white skin was no protection against the clumsy violence of their fingernails, teeth, and insatiable lust. Reacting like any samurai who came across this tableau was not something Ishida did. He didn't tie up his *hakama*, didn't launch himself screaming, sword drawn, into their midst, and he didn't decapitate them with the lightning of his *katana*. Dishonoring a lady in this manner required a punishment more severe than that. He went up to the group of rapists in his shining yel-low *kamishimo*, with a calm and noble bearing, and spoke the following words to them: "Just as Amaterasu after the dance of Ame-No-Uzume-No-Mikoto was blinded by her own image in a mirror, so is everything in nature drawn into partnership with its opposite and equivalent. Gentle-men, you being here on this wondrous day, in this blessed outdoor place, doing justice to the nature of things by manifesting your pure love for this lady, who with her refined virgin beauty could be your mirror-image, makes me thankful and inspires me to recite a *waka*." That's what he said. And when they got up and came at him with raised swords, he didn't draw out his own, but brought his calligraphy brush out from the sleeve of his *kamishimo*. Just as an angry tornado can gain no purchase on a gently wafting young reed stem, so his dances avoided their attacks. And like a willow sprig that's been angrily struck away from the path lashes back and welts the face, Ishida unmanned three robbers with his superior technique, inscribing the character for love three times with the brush he was using as a sword. After they'd run away, howling like puppies toward a short and miserable life, he took Michiko in his arms, nursed her wounds, carried her to Castle Oshi in the Musashi province, and married her without asking the Takedas for a dowry. The character for love occurs three times in the famous poem he wrote years later upon her death. In the original calligraphic text, those who take the trouble to study the minutest details can see that each of the three characters is drawn in a fast, powerful stroke, but there's a subtle and scarcely noticeable difference in the movement each time.

In order to create an unbridgeable distance, one should not insult with the blunt power of the sword but with the inimitable elegance of the brush. The man who speaks with the mild and soft voice of civilization instantly swipes the weapons from his opponent's hands—every angry word counts as proof of the other's helpless inferiority. Some of the best insulters I know accompany their piercingly soft sentences with superior ironic smiles. Although they generally achieve a satisfying result with this, I'm of the opinion that there's danger in this facial expression. Irony is an essential ingredient of the successful insult, it's true, but the most effective form of irony is like a low-flying stealth bomber that remains invisible to enemy radar. It is better to offend with an open expression of politeness, friendliness, and charity.

The most important thing is that the true insult shows creativity; it can't just be a random string of references to excrement and sexual organs. And just as the best style is quotable, the best insult has an aphoristic quality that does not just insult the victim but also, as an ultimate humiliation, renders him superfluous, so that the brio of the formulation of the insult outlasts the name of the victim. The renowned critic, Woulter Parr, was a master in this. The last paragraph of his review of one of K. Horvath's plays engraved itself in my memory after a single reading: "This is no play to be lightly shoved aside, but one that deserves to be thrown with great force. The stage set was lovely, but the actors kept standing in front of it. It was a performance in which all of the actors clearly and intelligibly articulated their lines, alas. Kitty Becker, in the lead, exploited the whole range of emotions from A to B. One would have to have a heart of stone not to watch her suicide at the end of the play without bursting out laughing. I never forget a face, but in the case of Kitty Becker I'm happy to make an exception. *Giving Hands* is the type of play that gives failure a bad name. The only original idea about art ever to come from Ms. Horvath's pen had to do with her superiority as a writer in relation to writers greater than she. First, God created the idiots. That was just practice; afterwards, he created Ms. Horvath. It was an act of mercy that God allowed Mr. Habold Sicx and Ms. Horvath to marry, thus making two people unhappy instead of four." You don't need to see the explanatory hand gestures or Ms. Horvath to be fully convinced by this.

Everything is always easier on paper, that is true—and I realize that now as I stand here before you gasping out my confession without the aid of the written word—but the ad hoc insult without an audience, man to man in the street, ought to respect the same principles. One often assumes one should be able to get straight to the point for that, and that's a talent you either have or you don't. This is only partly true. The spontaneous insult is an art, and, up to a certain point, one can learn any art. It's the same with the lethal martial arts I have become familiar with. A person who isn't intimidated by one's opponent, and who regards every lunge as a weakening of the opponent's defense, won't have difficulty finding chinks in his armor. And as long as you have confidence in your refinement and superiority, the most creative counter attacks will occur to you just like that. He who, in an unguarded moment, finds himself in a risky situation and cannot come up with an adequate reply can rely on three simple heuristic principles. The first guideline is the principle of contamination. One can say: "Jazz is music for imbeciles." One can also say: "Jazz is torture." But it is better to say: "Jazz was invented as torture for imbeciles." The second is the principle of inversion. Destroy your enemy by turning what he says around, or compliment him on his weaknesses and present your criticism as a compliment, the way Baudelaire said of Wagner: "I like Wagner, but I prefer the music that a cat makes when it is being hung by its tail from the window and is clamping itself to the sill with its claws." Another fine example is the compliment Will Rogers gave to the German people: "I must say one thing in favor of the Germans: they are always willing to give other people's land away." The so-called better than-inversion is extremely fruitful. People tend to say things like, "It tastes better than it looks" or, "He is smarter than he appears," even without malicious intent. The reversal of both poles of comparison can produce very pleasing insults, like Mark Twain's about Wagner: "Wagner's music is better than it sounds." The third principle is usually defined as an *aprosdoketon* and relates to the unexpected shift, to the sting in the tail. "Wager's music has its beautiful moments," Rossini said, "and its awful half hours." An even subtler example is offered in Clifton Fadiman's characterization of German nature: "The German spirit has the talent to make no mistakes except for the very largest." These three principles should offer enough support that you'll never be faced with a lack of inspiration and they'll enable the production of an appropriate and civilized insult at any time.

"There you go mister, sir, *voici* Belladonna, the Lady of the Rocks, hard hard, *wo weilest du*, the lady of situations, yes hard, yes *dûr comme roche*." She had fingered a new card from her stinking pants.

"From what I can smell, you've ended up in the gutter, and you're adding to its stench. I love women like you, but I'm driven even more wild by slobbering numbskulls with stale urine shampoo and shapeless trash-can clothes that nicely accentuate an abundantly shapeless body, especially when they could die of syphilis at any moment, or the galloping consumption, or a combination of both. It's an aberration."

"You gave me hyacinths first a year ago. *Quatre, mon chéri*. They called me the hyacinth girl. Four of wands. *Voici, mon chéri, regarde!* Here is the lady with four wands, hard hard, yes, *dûr comme roche*. And the fourth, that is you. And here is the wheel. And here is the one-eyed merchant. And this card, which is blank, is something he carries on his back, which I am forbidden to see. Sir, *schau das doch mal an, mon chéri!*

She really did have the entire Arcana floating around in her piss-pants. She waved one stinky card after the other under my nose, as if she were intoxicating wealthy women in the perfumery on the first floor of the Treviso department store with sample perfumes on white bits of paper. She didn't know when to stop, she was going too far. It was time to draw the line.

"*Síbylla, tí théleis?* If, instead of wasting precious time thumbing astrological porn and peeing on third-hand camping clothes, you'd received an education and learned Greek, you would have known how to answer this question. And when I heard your answer I'd completely agree with you, and, above all, I'd be very pleased to assist you personally with the realization of this ambition, if it weren't for the pernicious laws of this country. Now that I've heard the unparalleled wanderings of your words, you appear to be even more feeble-minded than you look—which truly can be called an impressive achievement—I am forced to put you out of your misery in another way. Madam, you flatter me with your attention but I don't think we would make a very good couple. A lady of your caliber deserves a man with more charisma, a lover with a delicate nose, equal to your perfume."

"*Mais non, mon chéri, sterbe nicht, pas ça.* It is more white than dead. *Wo weilest du? Cumis ego ipse oculis meis vidi in ampulla pendere, et cum illi pueri dicerent.* Cannot find, cannot find, cannot find the hanged man, *oed' und leer das Meer.* I will show you fear in a handful of dust. Fear, *mein irisches Kind,* fear blame, sir, blame the wands."

"And now that's it, bitch! Fuck off with your feeble-minded blathering and your filthy toothless mouth, stop grabbling around in your stinking piss-pants like you've lost your vibrator, you couldn't even find a camel in those filth and ass-scum-encrusted flubberflaps. I won't help you look for it because I can do without getting cunt-smeg and cobwebs on my fingers. You stand there stinking like a disgusting piss-bitch, I'd stick the whole pack of cards up your fat sweaty ass, if I wasn't afraid of contracting four hundred different dirty diseases. And you don't get a cigarette. And certainly not two."

She seemed impressed by my raised voice, and she started to speak softly and timidly. "*Quatre, mon chéri.* Her eyes were dark green predators. Blame the wands. I see them dancing in a ring. Careful. One must be so careful these days. Thank you." That is what she said. Or nonsense to that effect. Then she finally shut up. She gazed at me with prehistoric eyes that had seen more pain than I could fathom. Obviously, she tried to counter my superior verbal strength with a look of oh, oh, poor ignorant Rupert, and I happen to be the wisest woman in Europe. Poor Rupert didn't buy that, of course. Even though I wouldn't trust her to see through the tiniest thing, she must have intuitively realized that her attempt at a tormented, omniscient Sybil-look had failed because she shook her head and decided to silently move away from me. She didn't even dare ask for a cigarette. Her retreat was testament to my victory. She tried to leave like a General who has his eye on more important matters, but she wilted away like a wet dog on a Wednesday morning.

2 There are two kinds of squares in this world: good ones and bad ones. Fredo Square is a good one. What makes a square a good square is one of the greatest mysteries on earth. It drives architects to despair. You can design a square according to all the rules of the art—the correct dimensions and form, the right benches and attractions, foundations, and flower boxes—and when it's finished it doesn't work. It should have been the city's sitting room, where people can go to relax on benches after an exhausting day and wind down. But nobody comes. Nobody knows why. And you can have an architect who builds a crap square, because he doesn't have enough time, money, or interest in squares, and in some miraculous way it seems to work. Nobody knows why. I find this fascinating. I've spent years studying good and bad squares, and while my research is far from complete, I have discovered a number of important principles that may explain how squares work.

Of course, it is of great importance that the square is located in the right place in the city. This seems obvious, but if I had a penny for every time that's been overlooked . . . The square should be the mouth into which all rivers lead. The streams of walking, working, and window-shopping people must all end up there, from every part of the city. Some think this can be achieved by placing the square in the exact middle of the city. But that's too simplistic. The square must be a middle point, it's true, but not so much the geographical middle point as the center of all the stories the city has to tell. The square should settle itself where the life is. There have to be shopping streets nearby, small and big cafés, museums and churches, side streets and alleyways, cheap and expensive restaurants, cinemas and theaters. That's why Place des Halles and Place Pompidou on the North Bank of the Seine are much better squares than Place Dauphine, which is in the geographical heart of Paris.

The fact that the square should be the center of gravity of the city, to which everything naturally rolls, doesn't mean that it should be the interchange for all the important traffic arteries. On the contrary, traffic kills any square instantly. Worst of all is when the square is bisected by the traffic. Place Saint Michel in Paris, the Dam in Amsterdam, and Piccadilly Circus in London are continually murdered by these knife stabs to their hearts. But traffic around the square's perimeter is almost as disastrous. The square needs to stay in touch with its outer walls, they define it and give it shelter. This is why famous squares such as Syntagma Square and Omonia Square in Athens, United Islands Square in Boros, Piazza de Ferrari in Genoa, and Trafalgar Square in London are not good squares.

The square is defined by its sides. This is an essential point and has a number of consequences. First of all, the outer walls of the square should conform to the laws of aesthetics. They don't need to be flashy, like those around the Grote Markt in Brussels, but they should be correct, pleasant, and clearly visible. This is one of the reasons that Leicester Square in London is not a good square. It is defined by heavy concrete cinemas and vulgar illuminated advertisements. Secondly, it is important that the square's embrace closes without strangling. When a square is open on one side it loses its intimacy. The square mustn't leak, for then it runs dry. The only exception that can be made is when the square is defined on one side by water, like the Piazza San Marco in Venice. The entry points to the square are preferably situated at the corners, like the wings of a stage. It's best when the entry points are crooked or comprise a corner, thus giving no long view that detracts from the square itself. In any case, the wings should not give a view of the stage. If these entry points are too wide, the square loses its coherence. This, for example, is the problem with the Markt in Delft. The streets to the right and left of the Sint Jan, and to the left and right of the city hall, are so wide that the square is draughty and unsettling. The Piazza del Duomo in Milan has the same shortcoming:

on the northern side it is equipped with one of the most charming types of side-wings, in the form of the Galleria Vittorio Emanuele II, but this empties out on the south-eastern corner into an access road that is too wide, particularly on the west side behind the statue of the knight. Thirdly, it is crucial that the edges around the square have terraces. These transform the square into an amphitheater in which anyone who pleases can go play audience or actor by turns. I cannot understand why some of the most famous squares do without such seating. The Piazza Maggiore in Bologna has the potential to be a marvelous square, but the show is missing its audience. Of course the terraces should never be situated in the middle, like in 1818 Square. The public can't be expected to sit in the *choros* or the *skene*. The terraces should distinguish themselves from each other. The theatre should have expensive and cheap seats, boxes and stalls. A couple of Italy's famous squares fall short in this regard, such as the Piazza Navona in Rome or the Piazza della Signoria in Florence, where the show's public can only sit down in expensive boxes and where the champagne and caviar are of more importance than a good view of the stage. Finally, my preference is that the terraces shouldn't cover the total circumference of the square. It is preferable that one side be reserved for a public building of great beauty. The Epidauros Theatre is a better model than the Colosseum.

The dimensions of the square are of secondary importance. Some of the best squares, such as the Piazza delle Erbe in Genoa, the Minth in Tolo, and the Largo dei Librari in Rome are hardly bigger than a village green. The shape of the square has to be right, but there are various possibilities. The three examples I just listed are all triangular. That is almost always successful, unless the square empties out in the corners like Spui in Amsterdam. But square-shaped, rectangular, round, or oval shapes can be good, if their edges are correctly defined. And complex, composite squares, such as the Piazza della Signoria in Florence or the Piazza San Marco in Venice, with her spacious L-shape, have the potential to work, as long as both parts of the square are exceptionally good. The only thing of essential importance when deciding the shape is the lines of sight. You must be able to oversee the whole square from any terrace, without having to turn your head too much. That's why the square shouldn't be too long—the spectators on the long sides will feel like they're sitting too close to the court at a tennis match. This, for example, is the biggest problem with the Piazza Navona. In fact, every square should strive to resemble the best on earth, Maria's cloak, the mother of all squares, the first and last wonder of the world: the Piazza del Campo in Sienna.

Fredo Square is not like that, but it does its best. When it's on form and happy because it's being kissed by a sultry summer evening, it can mirror the perfection of the Palio. Then it can stop looking and smile like a brushing bride who embraces you and is grateful and all is well. She stretches herself out comfortably on the soft bed of the humming city, blissfully certain that she is loved. Then she undresses without shame and shows the curves of her outer walls and the sparkling elegance of her fountain, while hundreds of eyes caress her from the terraces. And the passers-by give slow glances, and if they had to be somewhere they've forgotten it now. They move as though conscious that every step could be a kick in lovers' eyes. And nobody talks about hubcaps, employability, mortgage problems, or the Móca's race, but everybody falls silent like when someone is describing his dreams to a complete stranger, quoting dead poets in a whisper. And while the evening lasts but doesn't grow old, a spontaneous gypsy party might start up in the square, where the bronzed women are all beautiful and dance barefoot around the fire, but that doesn't happen, because it's not necessary—all the women are already more beautiful than that and the evening light trembles like an E-string. Tonight everyone makes new friends who ask nothing and speak true words that cause no pain. If you look up without blinking, you'll see all of the constellations from both hemispheres, because everyone is here tonight and not a soul is missing.

3 In the amphitheater of a good square, actor and spectator, exhibitionist and voyeur empathize so much with each other's roles that they can change places. It's a tango of the walking and the seated. The walkers walk or stand, or walk, pause a while, and walk on. They are either solitary or not, and they play the actors. Some of them are earnestly playing important roles, like the bearer of bad news who, with his right hand on his upper buttonhole of his left lapel and documents against his left hip, gives a carefully practiced rendition of not looking around, as he purposefully strides from one set of wings to the other at a certain speed. He is generally alone, but when he's in duplicate he usually doesn't speak, or only very little, with his reflection. Watches play an important role in his life. Because he's playing an actor who has no time to act and who looks down on all these staged frivolities with proud disdain. He wants to be regarded as a man of caliber who no longer needs to be seen, in the same way that a self-confessed femme fatale, with a scientifically-designed and fully laboratory-tested wobble-bottom atop two slumbering beasts of clamped thighs, is what she thinks she is because she deliberately, and at much length, does *not* look to see whether she is being looked at with sufficient hunger. And I was considerate enough to help her by imagining her sucking away in my lap with all that lipstick, my hand caressing away under her bleached hair like a throttling vice around her neck, the way she likes it, as she bends and twists forwards before the eyes of the city with the dripping orifices of a cow in heat. She didn't let her act drop but made as though she hadn't seen. She strutted out of the theatre, pleased with the performance. There are people who aren't pleased, neither at the prospect nor by definition. They turn up with a deep frown which, in a barely convincing manner, is supposed to convey some sort of existential indignation. They shamble over the stage without lines or direction and strike a pose which, with every gesture, radiates reproach at the non-existent director who hasn't bothered to include them in the non-existent script, which, in any case, is too incoherent for words. They are lost, and they act as though it isn't their fault. At unexpected moments they turn their heads to the left or right with angry, angular jerks and aim indignant frowns at random passers-by, house-fronts, or pigeons. But no one is bothered by them and no one plays up to them because their acting is so bad.

The residents sit on the terraces, on the edge of the fountain, or on the church steps. They play the audience. Some of them are really good at it, like that man enjoying The Raven's street terrace whose ostentatious relaxation is very convincing. Legs crossed casually, a slight smile on his mug, and hoopla, look at me, the dude in the square. It might seem a little chilly in the sun, but still lovely weather, mustn't grumble, shame to stay indoors. And the fact he's on his own is really not that crazy because he's sitting happily on the terrace with his beer, and, as it happens, he doesn't care what other people think. He's a man who knows how to live life—we can safely say that he's a cool guy. Perhaps he'll have another beer in a while, he's not opposed to that. The fact that his girlfriend thinks he's a limp twit and is currently having complicated sex with her yoga teacher doesn't even enter into his smug, happy feelings, since he's been thinking he's great all his life. She's probably called Yolande, but everyone calls her Jolan, or worse still, Jo. He calls her "doll" and has never understood a single thing about her. "Doll," he says, "My own dolly with her sweet lolly, aren't we good together? You just stay the scrumptious sweetie you are and we'll go on a little camping trip this summer to the Wagaland moors." But she doesn't want to go to Wagaland, and she really doesn't want to stay how she is. She wants to rove around Afghanistan on stolen horses and feel the auras of Tibetan scales with the energy paths of her vulva. She wants a tattoo of a Cretan axe on her buttocks, if only to sicken him, with his limp-dicked job as Cultural Administrator for the Minorities

Commission of Minair Center-North, and be proud of it too. "Doll," he says, "at least I know how to enjoy life. You should take a page out of my book." He should know, the limp twit, not man enough to even dream of fast cars or expensive Italian made-to-measure suits. Swami Albert is the only one who calls her Yolande, and he know that it means "White Lily of the Thousand Sighs" in one of those languages that are full of Eastern wisdom. She doesn't believe any of his esoteric bullshit, but that's no reason not to receive the divine rod of Shiva's creative yang energy into the heavenly lips of her white lily of a thousand yin sighs. And you can say what you like about energy paths and pressure points but swami Albert even knows how to find anal sites her smug trance-inducing cultural administrator wouldn't know existed. If only he'd cheat on her properly, with a blonde tart on top of the photocopier, then she might be able to rustle up a grain of respect for him. But he's too limp for even that.

He's wearing a sweater of indeterminate color. It's such a typical, ordinary, comfortable sweater for a man to be wearing, a man who, in any case, doesn't care what people think. I hate men who wear comfy sweaters. It's an arresting demonstration of farmerly freshness of the kind that, all dogmatic apple cheeks, feels sorry for you because you're too uptight and inhibited to dress properly. When you go to the house of someone who's like that, you can be dying of cold and still the heat won't be turned up. You should have worn one of those comfy sweaters too. And then the way he calls for the waitress. Sprawling backwards in that wicker chair with his really quite tight buttocks, for his age, in his baggy jeans, like he owns the terrace, he turns half-around to make a floppy hand gesture, as if he has special privileges here because he's known the waitress for years and she thinks he's a nice guy who calls her doll. But of course he doesn't know the waitress, and she pays no special attention to him. Look, now he's going to act as if he really doesn't mind—he knows she's new, and he's sure she's going to find him just as nice as the other girls do. And there you go, bingo, what did I say? A bit of relaxed chitchat, what are you studying then, oh great, innocent bit of fun, but what do you want to order, pour me another one of these yellow lads, lovely weather isn't it, alright maybe not, I could sit here for hours. All we need is for him to tap her casually on the thigh or wrap his arm loosely around her hips. I hate men who just casually touch girls without any so-called ulterior motives.

It's an arresting demonstration of relaxed, whistling worldliness, the kind that feels sorry for you, all dogmatic smiles because you're so uptight and inhibited that you think about fucking whenever you have any physical contact with a woman. But meanwhile, they're seducing those girls they've just touched in a normal, healthy way, while you're standing by; you don't need to tell me. And they manage it too, while you, with your genuine, honest understanding of all of their erogenous zones, don't even dare touch their hands, and you're going home alone.

None of this prevents him from gaping, with a look of shameless amusement, at a female item in red boots, as if to say, what a pretty girl with red boots on that everyone is looking at, they're wolves, you'll have to watch out for that, predators every one of them, have a sit on The Raven's terrace and open yourself to such things, then you'll see that a girl like that wants all the men to look at her, and I'll have a wonderful afternoon, I'll have a whale of a time, alright maybe not, but that's what life's about, pint in your hand and watching a girl like that walking around showing off her supple body, you can't invent something like that, that's humor after all, but you don't begrudge a girl with a body like that, because what she needs is a nice young man who doesn't sit drooling after every strumpet who struts past but who knows how to live life, poor girl, she hasn't yet learned what's important in life. That's the look he gives her. And that's why the twerp missed something that was really interesting: a young woman on her own who was so exaggeratedly pregnant that something wasn't right. The bump she lugged in front of her hollow back was so heavily set, and so caressingly supported by two sighing pregnancy hands, that it was unbelievable. She wasn't so much pregnant with a child as pregnant with the idea of being pregnant. It was the way those tramps in this city roam the streets with an empty bottle in one hand cursing through their beards, the ones who have been ridiculously generous with their special tramp perfume of wine and piss. The way T. S. Eliot was a madman who thought he was T. S. Eliot. The way Rupert was a madman who thought he could possess his dream. That's how she dragged that leaden cushion over the square under her sweater, looking visibly affected. It had to be done in several stages. She'd barely managed to make it to the chair on the edge of The Raven's terrace. She uttered a convincing sigh of collapse and that mysterious combination of unfathomable heaviness and blessèd knowledge. It was the sigh of a woman who was complete, and she bore her fate with the wisdom of a three hundred year-old angel. Mira would have said she looked like a sinking cargo ship. She didn't sit down there to look around, but to know that she was being observed in her role as spectator. She was like an actress climbing down from the stage and seating herself on the reserved seat on the front row night after night, according to the director's instructions, and the audience doesn't doubt for a minute that she'll get up again presently and return to the stage, if only because she's wearing a different costume than the average theater-goer. The waitresses don't even bother to try to serve her.

There was something sorrowful in her rapturous suffering. It wasn't so much that she identified with her role but that she practically believed in it. And it wasn't that she practically believed in her role but just didn't quite. It was that, from all the roles she could have chosen, she had deliberately auditioned for this saddened, tragic character who had to be played with naïve contentment. It was the fact she dragged her heavily pregnant self across Fredo Square without a trace of the rogue who had done this to her—and who would be a dim recollection as she served her life-sentence of responsibility—or that she wanted to display the crime in her belly to the city with such proud suffering. It was clear enough that she was the victim of a prick of a fuckrod who had had an urgent and passing need to piss into a bit of skirt. One of those Johnnies to whom it doesn't make a jot of difference, fourteen pints or not, he'd still like to tack a bit of cunt-face onto his flagpole, alright maybe not, but she was asking for it and he's no queer. She'll get nowhere with her accusations of rape, she was there and she kissed him, but before she'd advanced to the fourth syllable of contraception, he'd already pumped her full with a good dose of the healthy, virile Johnny seed from his ne'er trusty joystick, his best friend, because he's certainly no queer and he could have done it again, but he was fed up with the chick by then because that was the way he was. When he'd off-handedly wiped his penis with her hair, because that's something he'd seen once in a porno film, stowed it away behind his fly for immediate reuse, emptied a can of beer down his throat, said, "Well, hey ho," and walked out of the door, she hadn't even cried. She remained lying on the sofa with her hitched-up bra and wrenched-aside panties, she'd stroked her belly, caressed and fondled it until the evening light appeared to her like an angel holding a while lily, and she knew. She stood up, had a wash, cleaned the stains from the sofa as well as she could with lukewarm soapy water, and wandered out into the sleeping city, raped, happy and three hundred years older. She'd walked until sunset, without deep thoughts, a plan, or having passed judgment on anything whatsoever, then she returned home, made herself a strong Ïgmulg, and went to bed in her new life. This was her role—at last she had one. She'd take on this role as her inherent mode of being.

4 I went there often with Mira. We went regularly when she lived in the Alley, and when she moved to Manora Street, just at the back here, our visits to the Fredo Square theatre were about our most important shared activity. Arriving together on the stage was one of my biggest secret pleasures. As soon as we exited the wings and came into view of the audience, I'd put my arm around her shoulder, look into her jungle-green eyes, and kiss her gently and sweetly on the mouth. It shouldn't be the sort of kiss that would make the public think—dear me, my lad, what a passion, clearly only just met, puppy love, well, that won't last, I can tell you. No, it should be a discreet, natural kiss which would give the impression of not having been meant to impress the spectators. And the audience would be struck by it, and everybody would remember true love, years ago on a campsite in the Dordogne or in their home village in Abonk, and think about what went wrong. Next, and with an equally discreet and natural gesture, I'd wrap my arm around her hips and lead the divinely supple and voluptuously pliant Mira across the stage, and I'd know all eyes were on us. You'd feel the heated jealousy in the men's stares; the hopeless looks given by men in the company of their wives or girlfriends as the thought struck them that they'd gone about their lives the wrong way; the warm looks from old men with sweet memories; the warm looks from women; the amazed, chatter-stopping looks from the young women whom, when we walked by, had to admit, even they, that that young woman is very beautiful; and above all the smattering of looks of respect and admiration that I allowed wash over me like applause, an ovation for Rupert the Virgin-Slayer, the Charming, the Irresistible Knight, so noble, aristocratic, and great that a woman like this worships him. And one time I gave an additional serving, saying something funny to make her laugh and look at me like a goddess who was happy and had surrendered herself to my strength, wisdom, and love. Although our appearance usually resulted in all of the conversations in the theatre falling dead, some of the audience members added an evident *expressis verbis* manifestation of their awe, such as the builder who shouted after me: "Get a good grope in, lad, you don't get a tasty piece like that for nothing anymore, you must have golden balls." Mira didn't know that she was playing a star role in my play, time after time. She set foot on the stage like a spectator and walked to her seat without realizing that the show had already begun. I didn't enlighten her.

We would go to The Raven, or if our table by the window was taken, we'd go to The Mystique a couple of buildings down, and if the weather was nice, we'd sit outside, naturally. We'd sit there for hours and drink relatively little. We wouldn't gaze tenderly into each other's eyes, and we wouldn't cling to each other with the sweaty hands of people in love; that wasn't necessary because it wasn't necessary. It was a higher form of sitting. We'd read or invent the stories of the city being played out on the stage. Like good friends playing chess, we'd enjoy perfect silence or if we did say something, about a rook on an open file or a knight maneuver in the middle game, for instance, we'd immediately and completely understand each other. Hours would melt away into the game that was being played around us. But it was a more noble game than chess because the idea was not to compete with each other. We were both playing the same color and moved the pieces without rules or turns and with no other goal than for both of us to enjoy the resulting patterns and configurations. And the game was more noble than that because the pieces moved themselves. Our only task was to observe the movements and the kaleidoscopic multitude of configurations and analyze the possibilities. And the game was more honorable than that because there was an endless variety in the pieces: one with mismatched socks and a slanting toupee; one with a scratched out name tattooed on his upper arm; one with a bored woman who was much too young; one with a pram that looked so heavy it couldn't have a child in it; one with tight pants and a visible erection; one with an elderly mother who clearly had a problem with something; one with a normal, comfy sweater for a healthy young man who, as it happens, doesn't care what other people think; one with red boots on; one with his right hand on the top button hole of his left lapel and documents held against his left hip; one carrying shopping bags with outmoded labels; two friends who are laughing so much you'd practically think they'd just deflowered a monk together behind the fountain; one with a plastic bag that's just transparent enough to display a magazine covered in yellow stickers; one with a deep frown that's supposed to convey some kind of existential outrage, but which is hardly convincing; one with a pillow on her belly; one clutching a bunch of flowers like they were a medieval weapon for exacting torture and vendettas; one with a halterneck top and a back you could skate on; one with a long, straight pipe with a silver lid on top; one with three ponytails—one on the right and two on the left; one holding a mobile telephone that just won't ring; one with two watermelons; one without anything like chest hair wearing a Hawaiian shirt open to his belly button; one with a philosopher's hat and a walking stick; one with a German book under her arm; one with a pancake with cream only the cream has been scraped off; one with a girlfriend who is obviously so beautiful that she has to be kissed in front of the terraces, sparks fly, and you think well, well lad, what a passion, must have only just met, puppy love, well that won't last, I can tell you. The pieces each carry their own story, if you're able to read their faces and movements, and our game was to work out the consequences of these stories dozens of moves on and to link these with the other stories that the ever-changing configuration contained. We wrote a novel together about the city in which millions of people shared the lead role. We let it play out and just sat back. It was a form of deep and true happiness. It was mind-fucking.

5 Ladies and gentlemen of the jury, you'll have noticed I'm tarrying. You expect me to lead you to Manora Street and the damned alleyway in the Minair quarter where I committed my crime, or alleged crime, and the fact that I am keeping you on Fredo Square for so long is beginning to irritate you. However, my reluctance to hurry the tour onwards, to those places in the city which form the most relevant episodes of my story, does add to my credibility—although I hasten to add that it is scarcely with this intention that I'm sharing the aversion I experience as I'm obliged to tread the memory sites of my double resurrection and my double loss—my only intention is to do justice to the facts, and I stress that, consistent with the facts, on April 13th, this year, I tarried on Fredo Square for some time before walking down Manora Street towards the Minair hills. I'd rather dwell a little longer in the topos of my happiness than hurry to the common place of my humiliation. And I must confess that I deliberately drew out our stay in the mnemonic site of my pride and happiness in order to tell you about my activities with Mira, although initially they may not seem to have any legal bearing. The reason for this is that I have an almost panicky urgency to totally and definitively convince you of the churning depth of my love for Mira, my martyrdom, my masochism, and my sugar-sweet, shimmering Mira. I bore you with my insistence, it grieves me sorely, but it is of the utmost importance to my case that you understand how much of my soul Mira had stolen during the short time we belonged to each other. She took up residence in the inner city of my thoughts. Whenever I go into the Rivelath, I see her standing before me in her high heels and she says: "Later, when I'm rich, I'll buy you a big present." In the Flower Market she asks, "What do you mean? Why did you take off your pants?" because I'd told her about the time I took off my pants for the Italian doctor because I'd understood something about a bottom, while all he'd said was "Take a seat," and she didn't understand and when I explained it she said, "Moron." One night she walked by my side from the Market Halls to Murdon Street with one breast bared because she liked to feel the wind on her nipples, but she didn't dare to get both of them out in case we bumped into anyone. In the Lam and Flag on 1818 Square she told me that she'd wanted to be nice for once and had called Marika on her birthday and she said, "Happy birthday, Marika!" but then she didn't know what else to say and there was a painful silence. And as she walked along the boulevard with me she looked out over the sea and told me that she'd painted the sea red during her art class because that's how the sea looked to her, and a year later she'd done it green because it looked green to her and the art teacher had said, "That looks better already," and she told me she thought he smelled like old honey. I hear our conversations between the mirrors in her sparklingly decorated favorite local, The Corona di Mócani, where she always ordered a cappuccino which she drank with a spoon. And I tell her about the time I was on my own in a pub in London and I was sitting at the bar next to a cute, cool-looking girl with a nose piercing, who also looked like she was on her own and that someone wanted to take her stool when she went to the bathroom but I kept a hold of it, and when she returned I said, "I saved your chair for you," and she replied, "That was very thoughtful of you," at which point she saw the man who'd wanted to take her stool, clearly recognized him, kissed him in greeting, and went to sit down with him at a table. "Rupert," she said, "you're still an irresist- ible Virgin-Slayer." And then I gave her a kiss. Sometimes I talked about my past, how I'd let an empty whisky bottle kick around my room for days because it seemed so cool to trip over an empty whisky bottle. She found that funny. In a small cinema in the Latin Quarter an old film had her crying on my shoulder, and she said: "I wish I could cry in black and white." She's Polish and pliable in Gregory Street, oh how beautiful she is there. At the Old Port I smell her wet hair, because we hadn't brought an umbrella with us. No matter how far I go in search of her, I always find her. There's no avoiding her.

Of course that problem always cropped up, I won't deny it. It was particularly painful in the beginning. Various heavenly days of perfect, big-eyed togetherness culminated in a humiliating finale of ill-fated yanking and "It doesn't matter." To put your minds at rest, I can assure you that I did satisfy her, but it wasn't the real thing. She tried her hardest to give the impression that she considered my impotence a trivial matter, but I suspect she only did that so as not to put me under any more pressure and that she actually cherished the hope that I'd come to an awe-inspiring blossoming as soon as she'd managed to convince me of the insignificance of this, and, of course, this left me even more caught up in my failings. Over time the problem went away on its own. We hardly ever slept in the same bed anymore. Nothing changed when she moved to a new apartment. There were moments of naïve hope when, although longing failed to become flesh, horniness spread through my loins with a vengeance, making it even more unbearable. Sometimes we'd just be walking along and I'd well-nigh burst out of my pants at the thought of her naked body, but as soon as we'd rushed home and fallen headlong out of our clothes and my longing become flesh rose up before me, I'd shrink like a prophet at the sight of an angel. I was also firmly convinced that it would work at long last when I guided her into the City Center Hotel as my Polish wife. But we soon learned not to expect anything from those moments. We solved the problem by ignoring it. Alone in his own bed, Rupert had mournful sex with the dream of her.

But enough about the good times. Members of the jury, allow me to take a deep breath and summon up my courage. I will lead you to the place where I lost Mira.

6 Manora Street is a relatively narrow street that leads from the shopping street behind Fredo Square to Mocani Avenue, where it comes out at the level of the Treviso department store. It's an atmospheric street with reasonably maintained nineteenth-century mansions. Some of them have antique dealers in the basement or on the ground floor. But perhaps antique is a little too grand a word for the bits and pieces they've usually got to offer. They are more like worthless knickknacks people have held onto for too long because they are special reminders of something or other, but no one remembers what anymore. There are a couple of nice antique dealers in the street as well. Manora Street's most distinguishing feature owes its existence to some curious nineteenth-century town planning. To counter the noise of coaches, and through the mediation of influential inhabitants, the decision was taken to beautify the street with a sculpture, a monumental statue to be placed in the middle of the road. The size of the statue would be such that the gentlemen in their light, open calèches would barely fit past it, while the heavier vehicles would no longer be able to pass at all. The artist commissioned to make this sculpture, Beomir van Tolo, was given free reign. This was where the gentlemen went wrong, for when the statue was revealed it turned out that Beomir hadn't felt like producing the n'th representation of the magnanimous Saint Magaretha of Abonk, with orphans under her cloak, or yet another equestrian statue of King Randolfus the Reckless. He'd chosen to make a colossal, voluptuous, naked woman holding an apple, the forbidden fruit. The inhabitants, the mayor, and the aldermen all objected strongly to this monumental exhibitionism of sin in a public place. But Beomir saved his statue with a masterly stroke. He contended that it was not an allegory of desire but a portrait of Mnemosyne, the goddess of memory and the mother of the Muses. He added that he'd be shocked by a pornographic interpretation of his artwork, which he thought would say more about the depraved soul of the observer than about his artistic intentions, but that he was reassured by the knowledge that the counselors and the gentlemen of Manora Street were so noble and worthy that they'd hardly make the error of mistaking Mnemosyne for somebody else. At which the protests subsided, though the name Mnemosyne was carved in the base soon afterwards, just to make sure. Not that it really helped. In the local vernacular she's been called The Beautiful Lady to this day.

Mira lived not far from her, at Number 15 on the second floor. I can be brief about the reason she moved. The Alley was not bad, but she'd ended up there by chance when she moved to the city and that starts gnawing at you, that chance. You don't esteem things that have just landed in your lap because you didn't make a conquest of them yourself.

And for those who wanted to leave, it wasn't hard to find complaints. The studio apartment was awkwardly set up. The dark-beamed ceiling made a bad impression. In any case, she complained about that regularly. I had promised her that I'd get in touch with a real estate agent from Hestia Properties I knew, but nothing ever came of it. She found the apartment through Benno, the bastard. He's got connections through the literary circles in the city. The renowned Habold Sicx is keen on him for some reason or other, and those seen in the company of Habold Sicx have many declared allies to shake hands with and just as many enemies whispering behind their backs. This pleased Benno greatly, and, as a sign of his status, he even had a brown coat and a felt hat made. I've always kept a distance from that circuit. In any case, Benno was one of the first people I introduced to Mira. He was, after all's been said and done, the Amor of our love affair, for if he'd hadn't been so Benno-ishly pushy I'd have never gone with him to our student friend's party in Kse-Waga. Benno and Mira got along very well. They sometimes met up without me. During one of those occasions Mira must have complained about her living situation and so Benno had wangled something through his publishing friends.

And honesty forces me to say that her new, light, one-and-a-half roomed apartment at the front of the building, with a view of The Beautiful Lady, was an obvious improvement on her previous place. Anyway, the manner in which Mira procured her residence will be of little interest to you, but for the record, I'll state that in the spring she exchanged her apartment in the Alley of a Thousand Sighs for an apartment at 15 Manora Street on the second floor, in which she resided in the said context. And she didn't live there for long, either.

7 The afternoon was drawing to a close. I was visiting her without any particular purpose, as usual. We were just discussing things, things you'd have already forgotten about by the next day, until it was time to go and do something. That was at five o'clock. This gave rise to a discussion about what we should do, either go to one of the cafés on Fredo Square or to The Corona, which she also liked. In general, I let her choose. Sometimes she wanted to go and do something. Which I found ridiculous. "Do something?" I'd say then. "I don't really believe in all that *doing*. Observing is the best way of taking part. I used to have a friend called Giannis and you know what he always used to say? "It's no use doing anything because doing something nearly always makes it worse." "But couldn't we do something nice for once?" she'd say then. I couldn't think of anything nice apart from us going to one of the cafés on Fredo Square or to The Corona. From time to time she'd act all angry about it. "We never do anything," she'd say then, "you only ever want to go to the pub." But I was wise to the fact that she only wanted me to say that, apart from being with her, I couldn't think of anything more wonderful than being with her in a public space where hundreds of eyes would envy me for being with her. That's what I would say then. "Good," she'd say with a badly acted sigh, "let's just go show off." I always found it funny when she said that.

"Perhaps it's warm enough to sit outside again."

"No, let's not go back to The Raven. We did that last time. And the time before that. Let's go to The Corona again, if you so desperately want to go to a pub."

"What I want is insignificant compared to the eternal truth of your green eyes, Mira."

"Don't be weird."

"Weird isn't the right word. The power of your gaze is miraculous and makes me bow down in ecstatic oblation. I find it wondrous how the omnipotent almightiness of your eyes beguiles me and deprives me of my will."

"Stop it, Rupert. I don't want you to talk in such a crazy way. Not now. Not today."

"What's so special about today?"

"Nothing. I just don't feel like listening to your nonsense today."

Fine. She simply didn't feel like listening to my nonsense today. Another one of those moods. Just ignore it, it'll pass.

"My grandma's birthday is coming up."

This news didn't seem to interest her particularly.

"I haven't bought her a present yet. What shall I get?"

She couldn't think of anything.

"Maybe I should buy her some flowers. I believe she likes hyacinths. What do you think?"

She said nothing. Mira didn't seem to have any opinion about the suitability of hyacinths as a gift for grandparents. It was going to be a lovely afternoon.

"My tooth's hurting again," I said, because it was true and I needed something to say.

"Then go to the dentist."

Brilliant advice. How did she come up with that?! Poor, sweet Mira. She'd sunk into one of those clouds of indeterminate gloom again. I'd have to spoil her a bit extra today. I'd drive away those clouds with upbeat stories, apple cake, and my love. Come with me, Mira, I'll look after you.

"Good, so we'll go to The Corona, since that's what you want. Come with me my sweet tigress. If you're nice, I'll get you some apple cake. And if you're really nice, you can have some cream with it. Shall we go?"

"I've got to tell you something actually. I've met someone else. But you probably knew that already."

8 /Red torchlight on sweaty faces. A frosty silence in the gardens. Agony in stony places. Thunder rumbles over distant mountains. He who was living is now dead. We who were living are now dying. Here is no water but only rock. Rock and no water. And the sandy road winding among the mountains, mountains of rock without water, if there were water we should stop and drink, we can't stop or think amongst the rock, our sweat has dried and our feet sink away into this dusty sea of compass-less ploughing, biting circles in the prospect-less sand—if only there was water in these rocks, this dead mountain, mouth full of pent up teeth that cannot spit. Here one can neither stand nor lie nor sit. There is not even silence in the mountains, only dry, sterile thunder without rain. There is not even solitude in the mountains, but sullen red faces that sneer and snarl from the doorways of mud-cracked huts. If there were water. Who is the third who walks always beside you? When I count, there are only you and I together. But when I look ahead up the sandy road, there is always another one walking beside you. What is that sound high in the air? Who are those hooded hordes swarming over the endless plains? Cracks burst in the violet air. Towers fall. Jerusalem, Athens, Alexandria, the walls come tumbling down. Unreal city, far over the mountains now, the mountains without water to think. If there were water, but there is nothing but rock and sand in the mouth that cannot spit. The Rivelath bridge is falling down, falling down, falling down. St. Eustatius's spire is falling down. The turrets of the Belaus Church are falling down, and

Thomas tumbles in disbelief onto the Liar's Palace. The ruins of the dead city are far away now, miles away, over the impassable mountains of rock and sand, scornful red faces and the reverberation of thunder.

Ladies and gentlemen of the jury, Rupert didn't probably know it already. Worse still, Rupert the Hopelessly Happy didn't have a clue. Drowsing glowsingly in the robin red cushions of an ivory gondola that floated amongst flowering water lilies in a crystal clear lake in the land of dreams, he was hit by lightning and battened himself to the wreckage in the seething water of an angry ocean that washed endless waves of salty, silty despair into his mouth, cutting off his breath, his cries, and his thoughts. Gliding and sliding on silken sails through the cool air, high above the Persian palaces, he was hit by lightning, fell to earth with broken wings, and found himself back in the shimmering sands of an endless desert, no horizon, no life, no prospect of rescue. We can confidently say that Rupert was thrown completely off his axis by this announcement.

The question of how to react to this painful news raised its head immediately. That was not as easy as it seemed. To be honest, I didn't have a clue. The only thing I could think was that if I denied it, it might not be true. I wanted to turn the clock back ten seconds and stop it for all eternity at the moment just before her announcement. Actually, I didn't think anything. That's not true either, because I thought a hundred inane things all at once. I thought: no, not you, you no, it's almost five o'clock, it's unfair, I must do something, we're about to go to The Raven, it's quiet in the gardens, my grandma's birthday is coming up, the St. Pierre filets she cooked were disappointing, it isn't fair, it's really quiet in the gardens, her intrusive clock is ticking much too loudly, it might even be warm enough to sit outside, I must do something, I need to buy hyacinths for my grandma, my tooth is hurting again, or perhaps we can go back to The Corona again, I need to check if I've got enough tobacco, how quiet it is, her fucking clock is hammering nails into my head, I must do something, I must do something. And while all these and other thoughts were flashing through my mind like a fast-cut video clip, another part of me thought: if I hadn't heard it, it wouldn't be true. And my mind's captain, the director of my thoughts, made feverish attempts to find a script for my reaction, but he'd completely lost control of his crew.

I needed to take a stance. When people are struck by extreme emotions, they don't react sincerely but follow the pattern of the type of reaction that seems the most suitable at the time. They don't burst out with anger or sorrow, but are angry and sorrowful if they think it's appropriate because that's how it was in the film they saw. This is true of me, at least. The only egress from this turbulent deadlock, in which I could neither speak nor remain silent, was to find the right scenario for the situation— the boy is told by the girl that he loves above all else that she's found someone else. I reviewed the possibilities. I decided against a more primal reaction, such as punching her in the face or pulling her out of the room by her hair and throwing her down the stairs, since it would probably not increase the chances of her repenting. Giving her a distinguished slap on the cheek was also an option I rejected. That would seem old-fashioned. The scenario of an impressive, stormy anger that would raze over my beloved with the strength of a tornado, uprooting her, whereby, after a few minutes silence, she'd throw herself around my neck weeping, kissing me and whispering: "I didn't know you loved me so much, I'm so sorry. I should never have done it, I'm sorry, Rupert, can you forgive me? Will you please forgive me?" Upon which I'd hide my feelings of triumph under a mask of deep hurt and say: "I'm not sure if I can." At which point she'd start to cry even louder and say: "Please Rupert, try to forgive me, I might not be worthy of you but I can't live without you, I'm so sorry that I hurt you, how could I have done that, please forgive me, Rupert, I'll do anything to make it up to you." At which I'd say, secretly celebrating behind a mask of impressive self-control: "Alright then, I'm prepared to give you another chance, although it will be a long time before I'm over this, if ever"—this scenario seemed like an attractive alternative, but had, on closer inspection, a number of problematic aspects. Acting out my reactions to her shock was simple enough, but the pivotal point was the initial anger that would cause this shock. I could dredge up a few phrases from films I'd seen, such as "I didn't deserve this," "You've really disappointed me," "It's not fair," "After everything I've done for you," and a few more in the same vein, but there was too little information to put together a convincing tidal wave. No, anger has never been my strongest emotion, and I wouldn't want to play something I'm not good at. It would be better to choose a role that made use of my strengths. So I chose the script on dignity. I'd listen to her with monumental calm and self-control, during which time it was really important to allow just the right glimpse of the storm underneath the surface, because only this would give the calm and self-control its monumental allure. She'd be impressed by my power and control and my noble calm. It probably wouldn't have an immediate effect, but it would set her thinking. And these thoughts would ferment and become astonishment. And this astonishment would ripen into a renewed and deepened realization of her love for me. She wouldn't return to Rupert because she'd panicked at the sight of his pain but because she'd realized that true love existed, for once and for all, a higher form of love for the last noble knight, while her foolish flirtation would be nothing more than a slight scratch on his armor.

9 "Oh," I said, more quietly than I'd wanted. I tried to look at her but couldn't manage it.

"Don't you want to know who it is?" she asked.

"Who is it then?"

"I can't say."

"Why not?"

"It's Benno."

Benno. Of all people, my friend, the biggest bastard of them all. I stared out of the window. The Beautiful Lady stared back. I was playing a wooden part in an appallingly slow English film. The set was over-lit and the décor was too realistic. The acting was completely naturalistic, but the dialogue was from another world. I wanted to run away, smoking and wearing a French raincoat, to a muggy black and white scene, but I was stuck on the screen and I couldn't give myself a third dimension. Benno. If only it had been a Russian sailor or a Caribbean limbo dancer, then I could have come to terms with it. Or not, probably not. But Benno, with his brown jacket, felt hat, and his oh so fabulously interesting contacts, my fellow student, the friend who thought we should go much further in life, the man with the big mouth, Benno and Mira, my Mira, my sugar-sweet, shimmering Mira, no, I couldn't take that. I couldn't tolerate it, I couldn't permit it, I couldn't bear it, I couldn't stand it, I couldn't put up with it, and I didn't want it to be like this. It couldn't be like this. And above all, it was so impractical. I'd have to talk through it with him later, as good friends, what a hassle. Russian sailors can be suppressed. Or, if necessary, you can let them loom up anonymously in your thoughts from time to time and let black clouds blow over your face, to suggest suffering and give you the appearance of depth. But when your girlfriend cheats on you with a friend, there's no suppressing it because your friend knows about it. You've lost the armor that accompanied your role as miraculously happy Mira-lover, because there's someone who knows and thinks yeah-yeah. Soon, in a couple of weeks, when it's blown over, there will be talk of a Benno, who'll suddenly tell somebody that Rupert, shhh, but apparently not because Mira, ah-haaa, oh boy, and don't tell anyone else OK? And how will Rupert ever sit quietly in the pub again as dignified as a samurai, knowing he's being marveled at by everyone who knows Mira?

"How long has it been going on?"

"A while."

"How long is a while?"

"Just a while."

"Have you done it with Benno?"

"What?"

"It. With Benno."

"What kind of a question is that?! Why do you want to know? Is that the first thing you think of? You think you're a big guy, do you?"

"I just want to know. I think I've a right to it, to know that is."

"I'm not saying."

"Bitch."

She inflamed me. She had dark green eyes that shone like the gaze of a predator in the jungle. She'd tear me apart with her cotton wool claws and honeyed jaws. Go on, Mira, finish me off, I'm your prey, release me from my suffering. My last word hung above the room like the heavy, damp air of a rainforest. Her whole room was a bitch. The clock ticked. She looked angry. God, she was beautiful.

"OK then, if you must know, yes, I did it with him. It. With Benno. Are you happy now?"

The secret service of one of the technologically advanced nations had invented a futuristic weapon that, at that precise moment, was being tested from a safe house on the other side of Manora Street and had been fired at my back. It was a kind of ultrasonic phaser that made ingenious use of changing sub-space frequencies to inject a small army of nano-robot soldiers into the target's bloodstream. These microscopic, mechanical little lobsters dispersed with unbelievable speed throughout the entire body of the victim. The first wave consisted of millions of commando robots who raced up and down on razor-blade caterpillar tracks, backwards and forwards, just under the skin of the vertebral column, as quickly as possible. At head level, a regiment broke off and spread underneath the entire scalp area. Upon orders from the supreme command, they all began to pull on hairs from the inside. Another unit immediately set about disconnecting all communication systems by making a dull hissing sound in the ears which caused dizziness. In the meantime, central command was attacked by elite troops who rendered any form of thought impossible by spinning the brain around in the skull. Special military engineering troops worked away at the nervous system by overloading it with an impossible rally of meaningless and contradictory orders. The victim started to tremble impulsively in places he usually couldn't move. A marine unit poisoned the salivary glands with a hydrophilic chemical substance that dried up the mouth in mere seconds. Next, the attacking troops occupied the whole body and controlled it from strategic positions under the skin. Everywhere—on the soles of the feet, in the nostrils, at the back of the knees, the earlobes, the palms of the hands, the top lip, shoulder blades, between the toes—chain reactions of electrical discharges were set off to induce a state of total paralysis in the victim.

Done. It. With Benno. Mira and Benno. It. Done. The thought of this was acid and it burned through my whole body. And this irritation stripped me of the ability to think. There was nothing left of Rupert but body, and the body burned, and the fire was her fiery red hair that Benno had stroked; the dark green eyes she closed in satisfaction; the snowy neck that Benno had kissed; her shoulders, her perfect shoulders, carved from Parian marble by a goddess with a cobweb chisel, touched and desecrated by sweaty, ignorant hands; her breasts, my god, her breasts which aren't breasts but secret temples of whispering worship for a another, better world of lotuses and oblivion, divine symbols of sweet, soft providence, used as breasts by horny fingers—the image of her body, her naked body, groped, be-slobbered, taken possession of by dumb lust, this image was too heavy to raise up to my brains and be neutralized there. It sank directly, undiluted, to my stomach. It yawed uncontrollably through my limbs.

"How many times?"

"A few."

"Where? Here?"

"Yes. And at his."

"Did you really go the *whole* way?"

It was quite a ridiculous question, I admit it. I don't know why I asked it. Perhaps I was hoping for an answer like: "Well, now that you ask, no, not really the whole way. In fact, not at all. He didn't know what to do and fingered my navel." Or an answer like: "No, you moron, he was castrated at the literary society's initiation ceremony." Or an answer like: "As soon as I'd undressed and stood before him like the embodiment of a dream, he shriveled like a prophet at the sight of an angel." Or perhaps I asked the question because I wanted to know what that dog had gotten up to with my goddess's body. Imagination is a more powerful poison than reality. My fantasy needed to be tempered with details. Details make everything bearable. That's as it may be, but in any case it wasn't a very intelligent thing to ask. She clammed shut and looked at me with an expression that hardened like wetted steel. She was gruesomely splendid.

"Did we really go the whole way? As if you know what that is! But OK then, if you must be so insistent: yes, we went the whole way. He kissed me and I kissed him. We French kissed for a long time, slowly, and it was lovely. And he undressed me and I undressed him. Completely. And we caressed each other all over and particularly between the legs. He was horny and I was horny. I was as wet as a sponge, and he had an enormous, hard, erect cock. I only had to stroke his balls and his prick glistened with enjoyment. Then he pushed me onto the bed and we went the whole way. He put his hard, erect cock into my wet cunt. That's called fucking, maybe you don't know that, but that's what we did. And more than once. And I can also tell you that it was nice. Want any more details?"

I saw it unfold in front of me. She, with all her shimmering curves. With her eyes, lips, and supple hips singing out yes. Her hand moving slowly from his middle to his buttocks and thighs, assessing its effects. She comes across a larger prize than she'd expected. "Oh?" she murmurs, and her hand caresses him like a summer breeze rippling through the grass and along the grain of the trunk. It's a balmy zephyr that encourages growth. He moans with the pain of a divine swelling and glittering, amber droplets flow from him. Only then does she begin to take him in hand; she grasps him decisively and with confident movements she purloins his essence. He reeks of man from every pore. With the accomplished might of a warrior, he pushes his prey backwards until she falls down onto the soft moss of his snare. "Oh?" she says. She settles herself comfortably in his power. He closes around his captured goddess, and he encounters no resistance as he pushes her thighs apart. With a quiet smile of desire, she unfolds the view of her glimmering, warm pelt that sings of longing and is a sea to drown in. He mounts the incline of her hills up to her lips, kisses her and kisses her, and while he kisses her he feels a hand guiding him, unmistakably steering him, urging his bedewed peak to kiss the secret divine temple where she is no longer human. Forbidden, he thinks. No man may enter this holy place. He closes his eyes, sacrifices his life and with a long, soft sigh lets himself fall. It happens before my very eyes. It happens in my stomach and it spreads through my limbs.

"Did you come?"

Her lips were pursed. Her eyes sparked like uncuttable jewels. She was no longer a woman but had solidified into a superhuman-sized marble goddess. She looked down on her worshipper with awe-inspiring wrath. She smelled of danger. I wanted to give up my life for her. I craved her. I plastered her with my submissive gaze.

"Yes, I came. Several times. Several times each time. I had fantastic orgasms, and he did too by the way. All over the place. In my cunt, over my tits, in my mouth, and in my ass. Had enough yet?"

I saw it unfold before my eyes. Mira lying there, sticky with pounding man-sweat, crying out with pleasure like a helpless quarry about to be torn apart. Her death cry shuddered through my body. She rode him like a nymph mistreating a donkey and, braying, he let himself be milked by her seething hips. His desire rushed through my body. He set her down in front of him like a pinball machine, put his fingers on the buttons of her hips, pulled her towards him, and threw himself into a tilt. I gasped at her readiness. She licked the entire length of him with her tongue, played him, bit him, clasped him, and he didn't stand a chance, she sucked him dry. He surrendered, and an endless stream of honey droplets dripped from the corners of her mouth and down her chin. I could feel her lips worshipping me. I couldn't do anything about it. It sank down from my stomach and took possession of me. It teemed through me and nothing could stop it. I felt the pinching of my pants. A hard-on. Rupert is with Mira and has got an unmistakable, real, hard erection in his own hard flesh and blood dick. I see her moaning body arching before my eyes and she's as real as in a film. And she mounts me and with the sigh of seven naiads she sinks down onto me. Look, Mira, look what you do to me. I undo my pants and my dick springs out like a young fighting bull. What are you doing now, she says. And she spreads out her creamy cloud-body for me, especially for me, and I moan as I force my love into her. Look, Mira, I've got a hard-on, I told you it was possible, I'm normal again, we can do it, Mira, look, I'll worship you like a granite god. She coolly circles me, and I can't do anything about it. I can't leave it alone. She looks at me like an animal. I see myself through her eyes. Tear me up, tigress, come and get me with your claws and your teeth. Stop it, she says. But she doesn't want me to stop. Look, Mira, look at me. I'm doing it. You've been fucked by another man and I'm beating off. You've had Benno's glowing hotrod in your frothing cunt, and I'm here watching it, and I'm jerking my cock off about his horny cock being in your horny cunt. You filthy pervert, she says, but she only says it because she wants me to go on. Look at me when you're fucking someone else. Bring your hand over here and feel how hard I love you. I love you, Mira, sweet, sweet Mira. I love you so much. Look what I'm doing for you. I'm venerating you. I adore the dazzling beauty of your body which offers itself to a dog. I'll make a sacrifice for you Mira, my sugar-sweet shimmering Mira. I'll give you what I've never been able to give you before. Look at me. It's coming. It's only for you, Mira, Mira, look Mira.

10 And she looked at me. She looked at me as she'd never looked at me before. There I was, Rupert the Unrescuable, fallen back down to earth, where her clock was ticking too loudly in a room with too much light, my hand still on my semi-erect penis and sperm on my fingers, on my pants, and on her carpet. And she looked at me, no longer as meltingly hot fiction, but as the congealing reproach of cold facts. It was quiet in the gardens. I was empty. Not a single thought came to me. I was in an abandoned city in which the only sound was the echo of the hopeless screams of the last survivor, and he was screaming out her name.

"So. Now we've had sex too. Are you satisfied now? Was it good? What a pathetic jerk you are. Now zip up your pants, get up, put on your coat, and get out of my sight. Jesus! So that's what you're like. I've seen through you, you're just a filthy pervert who gets off on dirty stories. You're just a bastard, Rub-off Rupert, a disgusting, filthy bastard. And now get lost. I never want to see you again."

Rub-off Rupert zipped up his pants, stood up, and put on his coat. He looked at the woman who was all the women he'd ever imagined and had worshipped a thousand times and she was seven times more beautiful than them and she was real. She was irremediably real and staring him out of her life with scorn and disbelief, as if she'd seen the Rupert who'd been hiding in Rupert for the past seven months for the first time. He wanted to say something memorable. He wanted to explain that she had always been the fact that had made fiction impossible. He had wanted to say that she'd shrunk him with all her unparalleled reality only to erect him again once he could picture her as a shimmering fantasy. He wanted to explain that he'd just played a role as he always did, but that it was his first role in her film and that he'd seen himself in his role being watched by her. He wanted to tell her everything about the lady of the seven times seven roses. He wanted to tell her that he loved her. He didn't say anything. He turned around, left the room, walked down the stairs, opened the front door, walked out onto the street, and closed the front door behind him. The noise of the door closing against the latch broke him definitively. The Beautiful Lady had seen everything and would remember it, that's what she was there for. Rupert no longer existed.

Honorable members of the jury, in my holy pursuit to fulfill my duty and elucidate every point in question concerning the reality and the full truth with regards to the circumstances pertaining to my crime, or alleged crime, on the April 13th in question, I have not spared myself. The story of my resurrection and death in Manora Street is no simple story to tell. I hope that you are prepared to grant a short adjournment, in order for me to regain the calm and clarity necessary to continue my journey towards Minair and to the most weighty points in the charges against me. In the third sitting, I promise you I will fully complete my plea and round up my defense. Thank you for your understanding.

THE THIRD HEARING

1 / The sun slowly began to call it a day. She was beginning to lose her bloom, her shift was coming to an end. It was high time to turn the city over to the twinkling of the darkness. She shot one last hasty glance through the buildings along the streets and squares and decided to draw business to a close. She sped up her pace. She was on her way to a well-deserved pint in her favorite local beneath the horizon. Tourists and city-dwellers followed her example. Little more was expected of this day. People began to work up an appetite for the evening and set about getting a foretaste of it.

I didn't feel like going past The Beautiful Lady. Usually, 1 experience a wry kind of pleasure in paying her a visit and nodding at her like an old girlfriend who is alone in her knowledge of my wounds. She gives me an understanding look and words are unnecessary. But this time our reunion left me less unmoved than expected. The image of Mira and my humiliation didn't rise up in my mind like a fragment of a painfully recognizable poem, as was usual, but sank directly, undiluted, to my stomach, where it did terrible, turbulent things. I don't know why, on this particular Sunday, April 13th, I was so susceptible to memory. I'd inadvertently looked up at the window of the second-floor apartment. I was sorely upset by this. I scraped off the memories like sticky chewing gum from the sole of a shoe and went on my way. My shadow rose up to meet me.

I turned out of Manora Street towards Mócani Avenue. A few of the antique dealers had begun to carry the items they evidently considered to be the most representative of their wares back inside. They were not expecting much more from the day either. They were wrapping things up early. On the other side of the street, a young girl came fluttering around the corner from Dulle Alley. I crossed over and matched my step to hers. Visibly moved, she slowed down for me. She was wearing a wide, long skirt, which must have been out of fashion for years, and she had a full, dark braid that hung well below her buttocks. She was a timeless girl, ageless, and she emphasized this by carrying her sweet smallness erect and proud, like a French countess who, through a combination of back luck and misunderstanding, has been dropped off in the wrong quarter by her coachman and who shows her true nobility by allowing none of her disdain and angst to be betrayed by her posture. I wanted to rescue her. I weighed up various strategies. I could catch up with her and speak to her, perhaps pretending to need a light, or that I was lost, or that I had no idea of the exact time. This plan seemed a little too radical. But just in case, I removed my watch and put it in my pocket. I could also collapse behind her with a great hullabaloo and permit her to tend to my simulated malaise. But the risk of her not responding to my tormented cries was too great, and I'd be left floundering on the pavement until I'd gone on for long enough and decided to stop; I'd get up, and only then would I notice that the shopkeepers had been following the entire charade. I decided to opt for the plan of waiting for her to enter one of the antique bookshops. Shortly thereafter, I'd happen to go into the same shop, and I'd spy on her from behind the cookery books with great cunning, to see which dead poet she picked up, and I'd address her with a quotation, after which I could seamlessly move on to praising her eyes in poetic terms. It was a good plan, but it failed. She didn't go into any of the shops. She turned left at the Borsteliers Jacket and entered the second or third door on the right hand side of the street. I congratulated myself on having obtained her address.

At the top of Manora Street, I crossed Mócani Avenue at the lights. The majestic Treviso department store towered haughtily above the noisy traffic and above the hundreds of last minute shoppers who scratched at its doors. It had the same kind of anachronistic nobility which the small girl with the long braid had shown as she towered haughtily past the city's concerns. I entered through one of the Egyptian doors on the north wing. Not because I was intending to buy anything. I didn't need anything, and if I had needed something, I certainly wouldn't be buying it here, in this stuffed and antiquated museum of contemporary luxury. I went inside because the marble halls of the Treviso were part of my habitual route. In this temple of availability, one could get a load of the loaders. Everything is for sale here, and the customer who manages to come up with something that's not in stock gets ten percent off the item in question, as a reward for his inventiveness, as soon as it is located, flown in, and supplied. There's a rumor that the sheik of Oman managed to get his hands on a pregnant tapir for a very reasonable price in this manner.

These glistening halls echo with the sounds of the shuffling footsteps of thousands whispering in awe. The blunt exhibitionism of the price tickets in the shop windows concurs with the voyeurism of the sightseers and luxury-lovers; here their shameless exhibitionism merges passionately with my voyeurism. I can spend hours looking at people who are looking at objects which stir up inextinguishable greed more through their price than through their beauty. Even the moneyed clients, making actual purchases and feigning a businesslike casualness while they regard the hordes of destitute gawkers beneath their feet with haughty exasperation, even they have a hungry look of unrelenting greed in their eyes. It's pure sex in fact. Pure bestial lust. The seductive wares in the windows want nothing more than to be possessed. And the people possess them with their gaze without being ashamed of the lasciviousness splattering from their eyes. The women in particular lose any form of decorum as they allows their seducers to entertain them. I like coming here.

As usual, I concentrated my attention on the hall of mirrors which twinkled with white gold, platinum, diamonds, jewelry, clocks, and all those other things that make women sigh with longing. As usual, I wasn't disappointed. A lady in a fur coat rode the display case of necklaces like it was a once supposed long-lost lover who had been deposited on her couch, brimming with force and bursting with abstinence. And the collection of diamond wristwatches was being raped by two young female tourists who'd abandoned themselves so totally to their crooked lusts that they were displaying their asses to the eyes of the city. I moved in closer for a better look.

"Excuse me, sir." It was an old man. He was standing behind me and tapping me on the shoulder. I hadn't seen him approach. He seemed very old, this old man. He was so old that he'd gotten over his age, in the same way that people get over their hunger or tiredness. He was tall. He was taller and stood straighter than old men were supposed to. His skin was impressively tanned, wrinkled, and cracked, like cowhide stretched over a medieval shield from an archaeological site. In spite of this, his features had something soft and helpless, almost feminine, about them. He seemed lost between two lives. Despite the gentle respectability he exuded, and despite his reasonably acceptable, timeless attire, I realized immediately that he was a tramp and one who wanted something from me. It's the kind of thing I notice. The Treviso doorman may have been taken in by his statuesque elderliness, but Rupert is not so easily deceived. That this yellowing visionary from prehistoric times had picked me in particular was testimony to a talent, developed and refined over decades, for picking out the man in the crowd who'd give in to his pushiness. He knew I'd see through him. But he recognized the free spirit in me, and in that respect he was right. He saw my calm step and open gaze as a sign of an unprejudiced nobility which doesn't hastily brush aside or nervously ignore the heterologous. He was probably going to ask me for a cigarette and then can you make it two.

"Συγχωρώ με, κύριοσ or, if you'll permit me to address you in the national language, excuse me, sir." His voice had a timbre that had died out centuries ago. "Would you do me the pleasure of granting me the time of day?"

Prefacing his request for a cigarette with an innocent question was part of the standard procedure. But was he really asking me for the time in front of all these watches and clocks?

I didn't find the joke very funny. But, on closer consideration, I realized that the hundreds of clocks and watches displayed here, and which, taken together, represented a greater fortune than a villa on a country estate in Abonk, were totally useless for finding out what the time was. According to the laws of chance, there was probably one amongst all of them which gave the correct time, but unless you knew what the time was it was impossible to determine which one. I thought to myself that there must be a good aphorism somewhere in this, but I couldn't come up with it fast enough. But still, it was a strange question in these surroundings. I looked at him to see if his gaze would betray anything roguish, ironic, or sly. Because that wouldn't do. But his gaze betrayed nothing. He wasn't looking at me. He seemed to be staring off into the distance, but his eyes were vacant. I finally realized he was blind. He probably didn't even realize where he was. This gave the whole situation a sort of tragic allure, something in the vein of a blind man who abandons hope and dies of thirst just ten meters from an oasis. It was also rather symbolic. Benno, the bastard, had friends who certainly would have used this situation as a metaphor for *la condition humaine*. Man's lot: ignorant of the time that has been granted him and ignorant of the fact that he is a blind man feeling his way around a temple where worthless time is being sold. Let's leave that to Benno's friends.

I looked at my watch. My wrist was bare. I started. I couldn't have lost it could I? My watch was nothing out of the ordinary, but I was attached to it nonetheless. Despite the fact that, given the rigid regularity of my morning ritual, it was highly improbable I'd forgotten to put it on, I tried to convince myself that I'd simply left my watch on my bedside table. It worked.

"Sorry, I can't give you the time. I've forgotten my watch."

"Ah, if there was ne'er a pine tree felled in the woods, if there was ne'er a groaning trunk stripped of its sap, if a man ne'er sailed over salted seas to a distant island, there to gather his pain and loss, though wrought as desire: his harvest reaps naught but pain. Behold this person who observes and grows at the sight of desire. Behold this person who observes and mixes memory with desire. Seeing does not avail him, what he sees is the guilt that cleaves to him. I've foreseen, predicted, heard, and suffered everything before. I've foreseen everything but seeing avails me not, avails me ne'er."

"Now, sir, it's not such a big deal as that, is it? There must be someone else here who knows what the time is. In any case it's getting towards the end of the afternoon. The light is beginning to fail outside. Would you like a cigarette?"

He directed his gaze towards the legendary islands far behind the horizon where something was happening that made him intensely sorrowful. Then he turned and walked towards the escalators, disappearing into the throng. Fine, no cigarette then. You're welcome.

2/Life after Mira was characterized by Miralessness. The days were usually okay. Sleeping in helped, even though I'd wake up in clammy sheets with a hole in my stomach. When the phantom pain became unbearable, I went into town to forget my Miralessness in the memories the streets and squares whispered. I took my habitual route and let myself be stoned by the memory sites of our happy times together, the way people console themselves with an intolerably wretched and woundingly bitter symphony. The suffering gave my step a calmness and nobility that suited me. I didn't need a brown coat or a felt hat to look like a poet.

Naturally, I'd tried to get Mira back. I'd been to her house, but she wouldn't open the door. When the door did open another woman stood there, a demon who'd taken the shape of my Mira. No, you'd better not come in, I told you I never wanted to see you again, and besides, Benno's here. Everything in her expression looked down on me, and Rupert the Reasonable of the "but we could still talk things over" shrunk into a tiny gnome with his own sperm on his fingers. He slinked off. And the time after that, she opened her window, and when I asked if I could come in she threw a bucket of water on me. "Here, wash your hands, you dirty pig. And don't ever come back here." Benno was there then too, I was sure. Benno was responsible for everything, that went without saying. He'd taken possession of her and had contaminated her soul. And the time after that the friendliest old gent opened the door. No, he didn't know Mira. Might she be that charming young lady who used to live here? She'd moved. I didn't believe him. But her bright apartment, which had once been a bitch, was full of the friendliest old-gent-furniture. Only The Beautiful Lady still remembered her. She lived somewhere in Minair now, if he remembered correctly, but he didn't have her address, he was sorry. Would I care for a refreshment perhaps? Something stronger perhaps? No, thank you very much sir, but I must go.

I'd never see her again, it was slowly sinking in. I told myself that it was better like this. I decided to give my loss a new name—regained freedom, that was the way to look at it. To make a start, I seized onto an old hobby I'd neglected during Mira's time. Almost every day I logged onto the internet to download hundreds of pornographic images to supplement my collection. After a few weeks, I was just as brilliant in my tracking down methods as I had been in the good, old days before Mira. I'd got my nose back for finding interesting, free sites full of very useable material, the ones which only remain available for a very short time in general. I spent a lot of time organizing the collection. Everything was saved in a file called "Samples" which in turn was in kept a file called "JPEGView." I separated solo from non-solo. The solo girls were divided between four files: Samples A-C, Samples D-H, Samples I-N, and Samples O-Z. I changed the original file names to the name of the model in question, first name, dot, last name, dot, two numbers, dot, and the suffix JPEG. They were saved alphabetically by first name. There was so much stuff on my favourites, girls like Alley Baggett, Aria Giovanni, Briana Banks, Chloe Jones, Cori Nadine, Elisabeth Ann Hilden, Ellina Giani, Gina La Marca, Heather Kozar, Jenna Jameson, Jewel De Nyle, Lexus Locklear, Neriah Davis, Nikki Nova, Patricia Ford, Peggy McIntaggart, Petra Verkaik, Shyla Foxx, Sylvia Saint, Tara Patrick, Tiffany Mynx, Tiffany Taylor, Veronika Zemanova, Vicca, Victoria Silvstedt, Zdenka, and many others, that they'd earned their own subdirectories. One of the most time-consuming tasks was finding out the girl's name when the scanner hadn't gone to the trouble of adding it and where it was hard to make out who she was from the context. There are various ways of doing this. Lists of the names of Playgirls of the Month in all the international issues are a good starting point. Those names can be fed into search engines which throw up visual material, and after a close comparison of physical characteristics, I could usually ascertain with some certainty whether the model in question was one and the same or not. This comparative method was frequently complicated by breast implant operations and other cosmetic surgeries in the intervening period, but with sufficient experience it's possible to eliminate these interfering factors. Another method of identification is based on identifying the series editor by looking at the original file name. For example, I know from experience that pictures with the file name "j" followed by three numbers originated from the producer Earl Miller. Via the various Earl Miller websites it's possible to track down the name of the girl. And there are other tricks. Even so, you're always left with tons of models who can't be identified. I parked those in the Unknown file in the hope that in the future I'd stumble across something that would relinquish the name.

I invested more energy in my non-solo collection, however. This was in the file "Samples X," which housed the following directories: Anime, Backstage, Bestial, Bi, Bond, Bond Lesb, Comic Strips, Doll, Dressed, Dressed Lesb, Dressed Straight, Enhanced, Hermaphrodite, Lesb, Machine, Orgy, Public, Public Lesb, Public Straight, Real, Series Lesb, Series Straight A-L, Series Straight M-Z, Smoking, Straight, Straight Hand, Toys, Twins, Vampire, and Xtreme Breasts. I used English words to give my collection extra allure. The series satisfied my furious appetite for collecting. I classified each series with help of the original file names in a separate subdirectory. I labeled each file with a series code, followed by an under-slash, followed by one or several m's and f's indicating the sex and number of participants, followed by an under-slash and my own personal typification of the series as a whole. This was often the name of the participating lady or ladies; in other instances, the name was derived from hair color or location. These files were therefore classified by series code, which is practical given that the reposts were often offered by series code. The most important thing is not to delete the original file names of the individual images if you're dealing with a series. If you do delete them, it's nigh on impossible to find out where the gaps in the series are and if the re-post you've stumbled across includes the missing pictures or not. In the remaining collections, the three Public files and the Straight Hand file were my favorites. Public Straight was particularly pleasing, but those images are extremely difficult to find and often of inferior quality as well.

Although the updating, organizing, and supplementing of my collection was very pleasurable, the element of human interaction was missing. I visited various chat sites and used ICQ. But it soon became clear that it was almost impossible to work up a hot-blooded conversation as long as I continued to present myself as male. All of the logged-in men wanted sex and all of the women just wanted company, and that's no use to you, it's the same everywhere. The only thing left to do was to adopt a female identity. The Real file in my collection had photos of girls which, with a bit of good will, could be taken for amateur pictures of real girls: photos without a series or producer name, not great quality, some of them dressed and the naked ones silicone-less. I could mail these pictures to the wanking men on the other side of the world if they fancied seeing what Chloe, Josée, Esmeralda, Karin Horvath, or whoever else looked like. But I didn't get much pleasure from it. And although I thought it was good stylistic practice to type a man off from a great distance, I quickly gave up on the world of chat.

Telephone sex was an obvious alternative. Occasionally, I'd be overcome by an irresistible telephone itch, particularly at night when I'd drunk a lot. Listening to stories or conversations with professional come-operators were wasted on me. I wanted real conversations with real fellow callers. If you're drunk, you don't notice that you've spent more time waiting to be connected than actually being turned on. What's more, you don't mind then that all the conversations are actually the same. Hi. Hi. Kevin speaking. I'm Angela. Where are you calling from? Oh that's a long way away. What do you look like? I'm six feet tall, I've got dark hair, blue eyes, a muscular, athletic body, what else can I tell you? Where are you, on the sofa or in bed? What are you wearing? Me neither. I wish you were lying next to me. What would you do? And the usual bragging about diverse sexual techniques. If you got that far. Because mostly you're cut off after the first hello. One time I fell asleep waiting. When I woke up in the morning, I was still connected. It cost me a fortune. One time I thought I'd got Mira on the other end. But when I said: "Mira, is that you? I'm not Kevin, I'm Rupert," they pressed zero.

All of this didn't yield much in the way of warm female skin or soft lips. Once, after her simulated and my real orgasm, we agreed to meet up the next day. I waited at a suitable distance from the agreed location.

From my strategic position I could observe who turned up. She didn't show. Or if she did, she wasn't as pretty as she'd said and I didn't recognize her. Or perhaps she was also standing out of sight in a strategic location.

Of course, I did seduce some women. I followed their buttocks down the street, stared at their bosoms in The Corona, accidentally brushed against their thighs in the department store when it was really busy, but none of them decided to kiss me or to go home with me. It seemed all those girls had organized a secret general sex strike and had sworn an oath not to give in to any man, however attractive he might be. Or perhaps they sensed that I didn't really want them but only thought I did because of my Miralessness.

One night, when I'd drunk too much and the telephone itch was becoming an irresistible urge again, but I didn't feel like yet another exciting conversation, I remembered that there was such a thing as an escort service. I'd never dare to do that kind of thing but still, I could just look in the phone book to see if there were any in there. There were a few in there. I picked the nearest one. I would never really dare to call, but it was the middle of the night, no one would pick up. They picked up. I would never dare to order a girl, but I could just find out if they had one available, because surely they wouldn't have. They had one available. Blonde, slender, C-cup, twenty-four years old. She could be at my place in half an hour. But was she also a nice girl and intelligent? Of course, very nice and intelligent. But what a shame, surely I couldn't pay with my credit card, could I? Yes, of course, no problem. I gave my address and hung up.

That half hour was hectic. First of all it, seemed hugely important to change my sheets. Meanwhile, I was haunted by fantasies of all the blonde superstars in my collection. They'd stand primed in my doorway on high heels and by way of greeting they'd clasp my groin, a hungry look in their eyes, like Sylvia Saint in the Suze-series fm-Blackman. I checked what alcohol I had because you'd probably have to offer a girl like that a drink first. In my anticipation of her arrival, the C-cup became more and more of an understatement. She'd ride me with billowing breasts like Briana Banks in em9801-fmmmmm-Boxing Ring. I combed my hair for the fourth time. High-heeled boots and stockings danced through my mind. I straightened the covers another time. Then the bell rang.

Gentlemen of the jury, I apologize for telling this story in a suspenseful fashion. The denouement in no way justifies this. Blonde was the only thing that was true. She was fat in a filthy manner, with tits like leaking Dairyleas. She was considerably older than thirty, with an ugly mug that dripped with stupidity. This was no Jenna Jameson; she was the kind of bitch who is baited out of her hole on a Saturday afternoon to go shopping at the White Pricebuster on Concordia Avenue, dressed in leggings and Swedish clogs. Her pimp did some stuff with my credit card, said, "Enjoy yourselves," and left. She sat her reeking, sweaty ass down on my sofa and didn't want a drink. "Just give me one of those nicotine sticks. I know it's bad for you, but we all need a little something, know what I mean?" God, woman, shut your stupid mouth. "Shall we just get on with it? We're sitting here having a nice little chat now, but before you know it an hour will have passed and you didn't get me here for that, know what I mean." I would rather have shown her the door right away, but that would have been a bit disappointing for her. And I'd already paid too. Come on, Rupert, don't grumble, do your duty. Get her to suck you off, then she can go home happy. When she undressed, it turned out that her clothes had actually been quite flattering, something that hardly seemed possible. She flopped onto my bed and began tugging and sucking. I closed my eyes and didn't know what to do with my hands, before you knew it they'd encounter another of her sticky rolls of flab. She set about it like a milking machine but nothing happened. Filthy whore, I said to her in my mind and it helped a bit. After that, I thought up things like: I'll fill up your filthy mug, but it didn't really result in the desired ecstasy. She went on to try to fuck me with that farting sow's cunt of hers but that was a complete failure. Finally, I just did it to myself. The idea that a bovine shopper from the White Pricebuster was watching me pleasuring myself was just exciting enough to squeeze out a half-hearted orgasm, after a lot of work. "Well, that had to come from a long way away," she said; it was the only intelligent thing I heard her say. She stood up, got dressed, said: "Seeya, right," and left. I stayed lying there, my hand on my limp penis and sperm on my fingers, on my belly, and on the clean sheets. Mira, I thought, if you could see me now, you'd take me in your arms, it's alright darling, it's alright, and you'd gather me up out of this sticky world and tuck me up safely with the cool breeze of your hands. This upset me.

3/ On the art of maintaining your dignity when you find yourself sitting alone for a long stretch in The Corona di Mócani during its busiest time. It was not my favorite table; two fat girlfriends were sitting at that one, one even fatter than the other. Drinking cappuccino, obviously, it was so predictable. The type that intermittently, and with exasperatingly long pauses, scrape a spot of boiled-on milk foam from the inside of the cups with their spoons and then absent-mindedly consume it as if it were a delicacy from King Fredo the Seventh's Court, served up every day to the same upstanding aristocratic guests who have absent-mindedly perfected the right expression of indifferent matter-of-factness at the arrival of sturgeon petit fours, peacock's tongue éclairs, and stuffed caviar. Those people are so criminal, winding me up with their tedious behavior! Ordering with their fat muzzles, we're in a café you know, or you can fuck off. They sit there with their monumental, sweaty asses in the best spot in the city, the sacred birthing stool of poetry and deep thought, the place with the most advantageous view out of the window, the eye of the world, and the view of the sculpted barmaid. They are sitting above the epicenter of the earth, where gods speak in sulfurous voices; they have no right to sit there, but they are sitting there as cool as you please, and they don't even realize it.

And then that so-called conversation they thought they were having. I couldn't understand them, but you didn't need to. They praised shoes and criticized friends. They praised shoes they'd bought and were about to buy and spoke badly of Miranda's shoes, the red ones, you've seen them in window of Mia Moda, heel like that, she's got no taste though, and they were expensive as well, but they just don't suit her and you know what she wears them with? No? That yellow mini-skirt she bought in the Foxxxy sale. No? Get out! With the yellow one? Yes, I swear, I saw her walking along yesterday with that new boyfriend she's got, what's his name again? Karim? Yes, Karim, that girl simply has no taste. She can't do anything about it, I know, but then you shouldn't buy red shoes like that. If she'd bought those medium-heeled boots instead, for example. Which ones? Yes, you know, the black boots that we saw this afternoon. In Shoe Fashion? No, not in Shoe Fashion, not those ones. They were nice too. But I don't mean those, I mean the slightly higher ones in that shop, what's that shop called again, on the corner. Oh, in Miss Wonderful. Yes, in Miss Wonderful, and not in the window but those medium-heeled black boots inside on the rack, they look a bit like the ones I bought recently, you know, those expensive brown ones that give me blisters, but then different. Oh yes, I didn't like those much. But they'd be good for Randy, they'd suit those long matchsticks of hers, but you know what her problem is, that girl simply has no taste. No, and you know what I heard recently about her boyfriend, what's his name again? Karim? Yes, Karim, don't tell anyone else right, but you know what I heard about him? No? He used to go out with Estella. But that wasn't for very long was it? No, but you know why? What? Why it ended? Don't tell anyone else right, but Estella told Nicole and she told Bar that that boy, what's his name again, Karim, that he'd forced her to you know what. No? Get out! But what then? You know. What then? Well, I only heard it from Patrice, who'd got it from Bart, but that boy, what's his name, Karin, don't tell anyone right, but he couldn't do it with Estella. No! Get out! Whereas Estel is really quite good looking, perhaps not a model, but I think she's alright. He could only do it to her from behind. From behind? No! Get out! Shit! What a filthy perv, and what did Estel say then? Don't tell anyone right, but Karim couldn't do it with her, and then he said I want it from behind because you're not tight enough. He said that? To Estella? You don't say that kind of thing. What a dirty perv he is. You're not tight enough, you don't say that kind of thing. And then to Estella of all people. And did she do it? I think so. What a pervert. And now he's with Miranda, the dirty pig. She simply has no taste, that girl, no taste at all, I've always said that. Well, she should know, she can hear it from me, right, each to his own and all that, whatever, we're not interested in what she does with that boy, right? No, she can do what she likes. Shall we get anything else or do you want to go? No, we can have another one. You fancy another cappuccino too? Yeah, lovely.

Members of the jury, you'll be able to muster up some understanding for the fact that I wanted to subject them to terrible torture, to break off those vulgar painted nails one by one with a very small, nasty little set of pliers, those walrus bitches with their disgusting chitchat and sea cow asses sitting at my table and ordering a second cappuccino and definitely taking another hour and a half over it. But Rupert knew how to maintain his dignity. He straightened his back, looked around with a gaze that projected self-control, a self-control that was the fruit of years mastering a secret, deadly, Eastern martial art. He moved the ashtray two centimeters to the left, to bring a balanced composition of the contents of his table, and rolled a first-rate cigarette with great skill. With a virtuosic gesture of nonchalance he flipped his zippo along it. He inhaled deeply, like a French film star in black and white, and turned his attention to higher matters.

Because she was truly statuesque, a sculpture of unreachable grace. I couldn't get an optimal look at her from my position at the time. Her *igmulg* machine was in the way. But each time she went to the espresso machine, she shimmered in my field of vision. May everyone with eyes that see in this wonderful, beautiful world order cappuccino, may everyone with a mouth that speaks order cappuccino, and may it take as long as possible to make!

The café was full, as usual at this time of the day. The chandeliers had been lit, and the hundreds of tiny lights that smiled at the memory of earlier nostalgic epochs, were mirrored in the Jugenstil glass decorations and the large mirrors on the walls, which over the course of time had seen so many looks that their noble patina was coated with weary omniscience. The sweeping curves of the walnut sculptures curled under the play of lights like exotic plants. There was nowhere where smoke spiraled upwards in such a beautifully pre-war way to the high ceiling as it did here. The echoes of all the conversations rustled through the room like a summer breeze through foliage and mingled in with the sighs of long-deceased poets. This was Mira's favorite local. Here, on the striped velvet of the sofas that had caressed the thighs of so many bored patricians' daughters, she sat like a woman. Between these mirrors, which shine with infatuation at her glance and do their utter best to reflect the most beautiful image possible back, she shone like a goddess who has shaken off her human form like a veil. She twinkled and made eyes and spoke about a thousand inconsequential things through lips misty with sweet, heavy wine. I didn't need to say a thing. I didn't even need to listen to her; I was happy to be able to flaunt her presence, nothing more.

It was not in the hope of seeing her that I frequently hung out in The Corona di Mócani during my Miralessness. At least, that's what I repeated to myself constantly. I missed her. I sought her in vain in the mirrors and found instead the twinkling emptiness of memory and longing. She never appeared to me here again.

Most customers clashed intolerably with my remembrance of her. Louts through and through, who had no inkling that their presence was a kick in lovers' eyes. If she'd been with me I could have made fun of them for her. But now I swallowed their unholy presence with annoyance. They had no right to be here with their fashion bags, loud voices, uncool suits, high-pitched laughter, and sweet, white wine with ice, and enjoying it too, God almighty. They should be chased out of the temple. Let me be alone here with the reflection of Mira's presence, flagellated by the whiplash of walnut self-reproach, with the barmaid who towers over me magnificently and who would want to kiss me if she knew who I was.

I slowed down my gestures. I sipped my beer gracefully and smoked like a high priest carefully leading a centuries-old, hushed ritual. I cast my gaze around with the imperious austerity of an Elector and the babblers shrunk and became my subjects. I let myself sink down below time into the dark region where all thoughts reach full maturity and materialize powerfully in the mind. I began to play with big, heavy words which I called up from the spirits of my forefathers in the hope that their resounding tones would offer me some deep insight. Nothing came to me. I ended up thinking about tits. It occurred to me that I lacked self-awareness. Perhaps Mira was right. "You always know how everything should be," she said, "and what everyone thinks and does, but you never think anything yourself. I don't even think you even have any qualities." I read the stories of the city and do some stuff, mostly nothing. A profound sadness descended upon me.

Someone deserved to be lavishly praised, because someone ordered more of that cappuccino that takes so long to make. Four cups no less; raise your voices in a hymn of jubilation. She really was unapproachably exquisite. She'd been erected from shining bronze. Her figure had been shaped for eternity. A memory of Spanish or Caribbean dance flooded through her movements, her black hair smelled of a warm sea wind, her shining black eyes shattered every man to smithereens. Her white blouse and her white apron shouted with joy at having been awarded the privilege of enveloping her, but she was more the kind of woman who makes the sand rustle under her feet and pinions the sun between her copper thighs. She is called Dolores, she has to be, it can't be anything else. She deserves a collection of longing-filled elegies, plumbed with pain.

Something had to happen. I had to do something. I swilled down my beer in a single gulp so that I could order another one. I choked and fell into a coughing fit. When I'd stopped coughing, a young waitress appeared at my table, took my empty glass, and asked if I wanted anything else. Of course this hadn't been my intention at all. I needed to order at the bar and look her in the eyes and be consumed by her fire. But of course, I couldn't now refrain from ordering only to go to the bar and order. That would look really strange and might even betray my intentions. I briefly considered the possibility of ordering something now and then saving face by going to the bar to say I'd changed my mind. But I decided against this option, thinking that I would come across as a vacillating type, and Dolores would make short work of any man who didn't know what he wanted, that much was clear. The only thing to do was to give way to the circumstances and order another beer first, before having my soul scorched by her gaze.

The beer took a long time to arrive. When it finally showed up, I tried to drink it as fast as possible. But then I realized I'd be making the same mistake again. I should save the last sip until all of the serving staff were out of range. I should also ensure that the moment coincided with one when Dolores was between orders at the bar, and her barman colleague was busy concocting all kinds of complicated drinks. All these diverse factors turned the drinking of the final sip into a complex and lengthy affair. But finally the moment arrived. The planets were in complete alignment, and it was time for the big deed. I gulped the last sip like a magic elixir for a hero's courage, stood up, and walked to the bar. Everything was perfect. He was busy doing something manly and time-consuming, changing a keg or something like that, and she stood there sparkling with availability. Oh, sovereign of soft shuddering, I approach you as worshipper, grant me a glance of your eyes! And as I approached her, I had an epiphany. I'd order rum, not beer, beer was for the thick-headed proletarians who hung around her without any respect for the revelation of the heavenly, who could speak to her without burning their soul, and who might even address her as doll. I'd never drink beer again. I'd ask for rum, and I'd say it in a voice in which the rolling of the r's resounded with the stamping hooves of my passion.

When I got to the bar, the phone rang. "Can you get that? I'm just changing a keg." She picked up the phone. I waited. I couldn't hear what she said, but obviously the conversation induced a lot of leafing through a big book next to the till. The book contained no definite answer to the truth that was being sought. After a number of inaudible sentences, she disappeared into a room behind the bar, which clearly contained the archives, or housed an oracle who could answer any question. I waited. The dishwasher looked up and saw me standing there. I avoided his gaze. It was no use. He broke off from his task and came over to me. "Can I help you?" It was all no use. I searched desperately for a way out, but there was no avoiding it. I ordered a rum without rolling the r. "You're not supposed to order at the bar, sir. If you sit down, someone will be along shortly to take your order." "But I've been waiting for ages and I thought I'd make it easier for you by coming to get it myself." "If you sit down, sir, someone will come to you. You can't order at the bar."

I withdrew like an injured samurai who is wise enough to disappear silently. I went back to my table, taking deep breaths of repressed bloodlust. It was occupied. Two men in gray made-to-measure suits had abused my valiant quest by taking my castle. They sat there glowing with self-satisfaction. I would drive them away with the flaming sword of revenge, and they'd flee like whining puppies toward a short and miserable life.

The only place that was still free was at a small table next to the bathrooms. By far the worst seat in the house. I went to sit there and meditated at length on natural disasters, suppurating skin diseases, lost loves, and death. I tried to catch a glimpse of Dolores, but this position was unpropitious to even a revelation in the mirrors. I finally saw her many lonely, begrudging beers later. She was apron-less and wearing a coat. She was leaving. There was still hope. Not all was lost. I decided to follow her.

4 It had gotten dark in the meantime. I didn't know what time it was. She walked ahead of me along Mócani Avenue in a northerly direction, away from the center. I followed her from a distance of about twenty meters. The streets were still busy. I could easily just happen to be walking here and just happen to be going the same way as her. I tried to concentrate on her buttocks. This was the first reward of the pursuit after all, that I could entertain myself with her backside and the thoughts of all the things I could do with it. She was wearing a pair of black pants which were really quite unexceptional, apart from that she was inside them. Her work pants, of course, I do realize that, but in addition to this it seemed to me likely that she always dressed rather plainly. Women with a natural beauty tend to accentuate their grace with nonchalant simplicity. She knew that kind of thing intuitively. In any case, her buttocks were fabulous in that simple black.

She continued along steadily, without being distracted by shop windows or passers-by, at the pace of a woman who knows exactly what she wants and is capable of. She walked like a woman who doesn't like to deviate from her habitual route. Her steady determination made my job easy. She was perfect following material. At Flehrmann Boulevard, she turned right. The road continues up into the hills of the northern boroughs, an area of the city I only know moderately. I followed her and tried to compose a poem for her in the meter of her bobbing beat. She went to cross over to New Bear Street. She had to wait at the pedestrian crossing, which necessitated some virtuosity from her pursuer. I feigned interest in the window of a car accessories shop while keeping the traffic lights in the corner of my eye. I managed to cross over at the same time as her without being noticed. On the other side, I slowed down to regain the right distance. I'm practiced in the art of pursuit.

She walked a few hundred meters along New Bear Street, and then she turned right into a street whose name I don't know. Here, the streets were almost deserted, which, in order not to rouse suspicion, induced me to increase my distance from her. What's more, I was practicing my I-just-happen-to-be-walking-here face in case she should look around, despite my caution. In fact, I hoped that would happen. "Indeed," I'd say, "I've followed you from The Corona di Mócani, which in all its centuries of existence has never beheld a more warm-blooded sculpture with its mirrors than the supple bronze of your provocatively dancing body. That's why I followed you, and for the black fire in your eyes that has singed the fields of my past and has left me as one prostrate, fallow present of smoldering desire. And I will carry on following you until I wake up beside you in white satin sheets under the late afternoon sun of far-off lands where you are born from the spume of the sea. That's where I'll know you are by my side. I will close my eyes and lay my astonishingly simple life in your all-knowing arms. Believe me, it's not my habit to follow women through the city. It's even more unusual for me to bare my soul to a stranger in the street. I'm not a man of great decisiveness. But when fate conveys itself unequivocally and imperatively forwards, doubt and caution are blasted away like lint in a whirlwind. It's not that I'm asking you to be mine for eternity. It's that I know it with the certainty of a prophet to whom the messenger of the gods has appeared. I will kiss you. Our life together can begin."

She transported me further and further up the hill along a number of streets I didn't know. It surprised me that we came out at Jaszka Way, which in my recollections was a little further to the east. But perhaps we were also a bit more to the east than I'd thought. She crossed over without taking any notice of the selection of seafood piled up in the windows of the numerous tavernas, which for reasons that were unclear to me were all adorned with bizarre names such as The Other World, The Glorious Sleep, or Crime of Passion. Her delectable buttocks bulged out with every step she took. I wanted to sample her. She went up some stairs to another street higher up. She swayed peerlessly along in front of me, a bronze deer, luring me deeper and deeper into the forest. The streets became alleyways and the alleyways became smaller, darker, and more dangerous. This was the Minair quarter, the old upper town which only a rare few know their way around. I followed her, letting the name Dolores whisper through my thoughts; I won her over with my eyes, and I contemplated action.

I remembered that I'd done this before. It was in a different part of the city, near the old harbor in the Latin quarter, but I'd once followed Mira in precisely the same voyeuristic fashion. It was a game, she came up with it. She thought it would fun to pretend that we didn't know each other. I'd follow her through the streets, remaining at a suitable distance, but close enough to give her the feeling that she was being followed. She'd try to shake me off, but it wouldn't work. And only once were in a dark, scary alleyway could I overtake her and speak to her. But I should carry on acting as if we didn't know each other and I should say creepy things like, "Hey doll, where are you off to so late, and so completely alone? Don't you know that very strange things can happen to beautiful ladies like you dark alleyways?" And then she'd give me a deep kiss. I thought it was a fun game, but it went wrong. Somewhere around Ennius Street she went into a subway station to shake me off. I tried to follow her but was thoroughly thwarted by the throng. I was distracted momentarily by an Amazonian negress who passed me on red, towering heels, and then I'd lost her. I took the exit that she must have taken, but there was no sign of her on the street. I ran back down, took another exit, but she wasn't there either. I looked for her for a while in the streets of the Latin quarter but I didn't find her. It began to rain. Then I decided to go to The Raven on Fredo Square. She'd certainly go there once she'd realized I'd lost her, if she wasn't there already. She wasn't there already. She turned up hours later, storming in, soaked from the rain. She was furious. In a dark, scary alleyway she'd been accosted by some dirty creep who had said very strange things to her and had grabbed hold of her. He'd wanted to rape her, she was sure of it. She had managed to break free, had run away and had only managed to shake him off after many detours. "And all this time you've been sitting here guzzling." I wanted to comfort her, dry her, kiss her, warm her up, and take her under my wing like an ailing chick but she stood up and went outside without saying anything else. I downed my beer and walked after her. I followed her in the pouring rain. I tried to focus on coming up with an excuse or something sweet to say, but I was drunkenly infatuated with the buttocks which were rolling angrily before my eyes. She waited for me in front of her door. Before I could say anything she gave me a hard, angry kiss. "Well," she said. She went in and slammed the door behind her.

The alleyways in this hilly part of the city became ever narrower and more fantastical. I'd never known there were so many of them. She led me along side streets off side streets, up and down staircases, past squares the size of a sitting room, through unpredictably winding streets, past derelict houses, through archways, up and down, and I no longer had any idea whether we were still going in a more or less northerly direction. This was the Minair quarter, a picturesque labyrinth with the scent of danger. I've haven't been here much. I followed her from a long distance. She mustn't hear my footsteps. It could no longer be coincidence that I had happened to have taken, from the thousands of possible routes, exactly the same one as her. I repeatedly lost sight of her, but I managed, after each turn and every staircase, to catch enough of her to know which alleyway she'd turned into next. I rolled a cigarette on the run. It didn't work that well because there were only crumbs left in the packet. Half of them fell on the ground. I was already out of tobacco, and now I was even more out of it. This half-successful one was the last I'd be able to get out of it.

The long walk through unknown alleys began to sober me up. Or perhaps it was the memory of Mira's wet hair dripping like the red fur of an angry fox. A sense of doubt crept into my steps. I saw Rupert panting over hilltops after a pair of buttocks like a drooling gun dog chasing a helpless fox, and I began to ask myself what in God's name I was doing. She was beautiful, of course she was beautiful. But what did I want with her? It would be nice if she'd dance naked for me on an abandoned Cuban beach at sunset, but even that gets boring after a while. Everything gets boring after a while, in the absence of green eyes to look, read, and invent with. And to smile when you say that she can dance well, and her bronze breasts swaying in the warm sea breeze like an eternally youthful and eternally simple song of soft scented maiden's flesh, and I'd like to fuck her, but slowly and beautifully for you. "Come, come, sweetheart, don't be afraid. I'm here. Fuck her gently, I'll hold onto you. Weep quietly onto her moaning body." And the sun set in slow sobbing waves that knew that there are green eyes that see how beautifully they undulate, that it doesn't go unnoticed, it is not for nothing and all is well.

When I turned the corner, she was standing in front of me. I almost bumped into her. "Might I know what's going on here? Why have you been following me this whole time? What kind of sick game are you trying to play? Actually I don't care at all what's going on in your head. My shift's over, do you hear me? Finished, *schluss*, go home. Go and find someone else to drool after like a dog."

"Sorry," I say, "I'm sorry. That's not what I meant at all. I have to find her. I can't go to the sea without her green eyes. I'm sorry, I must find Mira."

5/This was Minair where the city is old, real, and unfathomable. It has been claimed that her roots are here, that in olden times this city was founded on these hills, when there was a constant threat of danger lurking across the sea in Abonk, Ribon, and Wagaland. Others contest this and locate the origin of the city lower down, around Fredo Square and 1818 Square, where actual traces of the foundations of early Middle Age structures have been found under the houses on the Rivelath. The former do not dispute the authenticity of these findings at all, but they maintain that the focus on the lower part distorts our view. The rocky substratum of Minair that shamelessly surfaces here and there between the buildings, in the form of surreal stone formations, complicates the possibility of finding even older foundations—people who live on this type of ground have no need to use the existent foundations when they rebuild, they can build directly onto the rocks again, which has the advantage that the old stones become available for various forms of reuse. And if nothing can be found, it doesn't mean that it's not there, according to that theory.

I know this quarter too little to be able to settle the dispute. But the finely meshed network of crooked alleyways and even more crooked side streets made a really authentic impression on me, at least on the evening of Sunday, April 13th. That's something else people say: that the alleys of Minair constantly change form after sunset, so that a street that first leads onto Flehrmann Boulevard now leads onto a narrow fork with three roads all leading upwards. Some of those people whisper the story of Krisha, the dog who, in Fredo the Seventh's time, ran after a thrown stick and roams through the streets looking for the stick or its master to this very day. Over the course of the centuries she is supposed to have grown so thin that her bark is higher pitched than a human ear can hear.

"She lives somewhere in Minair now," the friendliest old gent from Manora Street had said, "at least that's if I've remembered it correctly, but I don't have the exact address, I'm afraid." It was a bizarre plan to search for her in this tangle of streets, but I couldn't do anything else. I was certain I'd find her, as long as I didn't think too much about this certainty which was being refuted and mocked by all the facts. I didn't even have a plan, but that didn't bother me. I'd find her. Because that's what the art of hope is like. People always claim that hope is important, that you must never lose it, and that you won't achieve anything without it, but they don't realize that hope is useless. What you need is belief that is as strong as the rocky foundations of Minair. The truest form of hoping is not to hope but to be certain. It's the same with the Japanese art of war that I've made my own. The unarmed man attacked by three *ronin* with drawn swords will not survive if he thinks: well, I hope I survive this. The only guarantee of survival is his own certainty that he will survive. This certainty is not based on facts, nor on his training in various techniques, but on the fact that he's trained himself to be certain. It is the principle of *ichi go ichi e*, "one encounter, one life." An orator who begins a witness statement, on which his life depends, without the support of paper, doesn't pronounce his first words in the hope that he'll be able to recall the route through the events and arguments, but in the certainty that he'll be able to retrace his steps. A man who defends himself against a charge will be found guilty if he gives the impression that he hopes to be acquitted. His only weapon is his certainty of his innocence. Hope is like longing, it weakens. Certainty shines with the bright power of memory. You shouldn't long for something but picture it clearly as a recollection of something obtained. That's how I pictured Mira, as I remembered her in Minair, where I've never been before. I'd find her. And if I didn't find her, it would be because I hadn't been certain enough of finding her.

Where I'd find her precisely I didn't know, but I didn't know where I was either, so that was fortunate. It was dark. Most of the alleyways in Minair are badly lit. The streets were practically deserted. I took a random street and tried to smell Mira. When the layout of the streets seems to show no planning and when the streets change position every fifteen minutes, arbitrariness is the best strategy. She could be reclining behind every unlit window, but I knew this wasn't the case, and I knew that I would know it when she was there. I quickened my pace. I began to think in short sentences. I was all senses. Snippets of music. Someone was playing an accordion somewhere. Mira doesn't like accordions. I turned off. The alley bent sharply to the right and split into two narrower streets. I chose the left one. After ten meters, the street ended in some steps. I went up them and came out in a square in which cars were parked. They must have been assembled on the spot because I couldn't see how any vehicles could have been driven here. I smelled a sharp, old-fashioned scent that I'd also smelled in Greece and couldn't place there either. Something of camphor and mothballs. It worked like a flavor enhancer on my memories. Mira appeared before me in keen focus, as naked as a statue of Mnemosyne, and I could smell her curves. She was not far away. She was somewhere in these alleys that curled around each other like her red hair when she'd just got up and was making tea and her bed was still warm. I was on the right track, I had to be, no doubt about it, it couldn't be any other way.

I turned into an alley which led upwards at a gentle incline, and I concentrated even harder on visualizing her. Because Minair rearranged its limbs in the same way that Mira turned in her sleep. If the city here was as unfathomable as a living being, I must handle her like a woman. I should use Mira's body as a map of the city. Then I'd find her. And I had to find her. This alley followed the soft contours of her calf. I walked upwards past the mossy, soft place right behind the hollows of the backs of her knees. There was an ascending staircase here. This must be her knee. There were four streets at the top of it. Which was her thigh? How was she lying? To the right couldn't be good. The knee joint won't allow the leg to bend that way. Straight on is also unlikely. Mira never lies with her legs stretched out straight. She bends as though her supple, pliant body is giving her pleasure. But how high has she pulled up her knee? Should I take a sharp left, or is her leg like a walnut arabesque over the sheets which are as omniscient as weary mirrors? It's late. She isn't rolled up like a hedgehog, at this time of night she's lying recumbent, open, and available. I choose the gentle bend to the left and it's the right one. The alley widens to her upper thigh, which I've so often stroked with my eyes, and the soft flesh my hands have so often kneaded into a breathtaking sculpture. I could stay here and worship her, but I have to go further to the dark green predators of her eyes—that's where I'll find her.

The alley dropped down to her loins. But something wasn't right. There was no plane of soft shuddering. There was no soft, secret forest that rustled like the fur of an animal being sacrificed to Artemis and that sings of longing and is a sea to drown in. They were just more stairs. I am lost. But I have no choice. I mount the steep, high steps and come out in a quiet, deserted square that bulges out of the city like a hill. No, I'm not lost. I recognize these curves. They are the buttocks that I've so often climbed with panting hands. She's turned over and is lying on her front. I cross the square and descend into her lower back where she has small hairs that are as invisible as the memory of a sea breeze. And she groans as I stroke her there and she arches towards me. I continue along a long, narrow alleyway across her left side. I hear laughter behind closed shutters. I'm on course, this is the right alley. Mira is very ticklish. The alley goes diagonally upwards towards her armpit. I'd like to fall off the city here. I'd like to tumble to the left and lose myself at her breast and I wished I knew how to cry, and she'd clutch me like a warm comforter and she'd say: "Hush now, it's alright," and I'd adore her until sunrise without stirring. Mira, my sugar-sweet, shimmering Mira, my masochism, my martyrdom, light of my lips, lymph of my cyanic sadness, sea of my swan dive, salt on my howling wounds, wait for me and let me find you. Hold me tightly with all the fingers of your hand. I want us to be us again because it was and it was good. I want to ignore everything that exists apart from you. I want to deny that things happened. I want to be you, I want to be whole, I want to be the sun. I can't read our city without the dark green sun of your eyes. Look at me and see how I look for you in every street in this city, in every conversation between mirrors in your sparklingly-furnished favorite local, in the buttocks of everyone I follow, and see how without you I feel so thin that my whine is higher pitched than a human ear can hear. Wait for me. I run as quickly as I can over your throat—which I hunger after like a snow-eating lion; across your cheek—into whose cool, satin pillows I want to sink; along your nose—a classical sculpture which pilgrims travel for days to see; to your eyes, the dark green eyes I want to be seen by, so that I myself can see and breathe. Wait for me, I'm coming to find you.

But this isn't her throat. The alley to the gateway of her armpit seemed too long and too narrow. And what's more it ascended diagonally. And here the alley becomes even narrower and displays a kink to the right like an elbow. Something doesn't fit. I should have reached her cheek ages ago. Her throat doesn't have a kink in it. I carry on. The alley becomes a little wider again, but it's still not wide enough. The old houses on both sides of the street close in on me and stare at me with dark, dull eyes. Far off I can hear a dog barking. Further on, the alley narrows again, and it's narrower here than any I've seen until now. The city grips me like handcuffs around a wrist. I wriggle my way through the alley and arrive at a small square. It's a five-pronged fork. Behind me there's the path I've just taken, and in front of me are five very small alleyways, splayed like the fingers of a hand. I have no idea where I am. I'm lost in her body. I chose the fork on the far right because it's the least narrow, relatively. The alley is short. I come out at a square I don't recognize. I can't smell her anymore, I've lost her. I'm somewhere in Minair and suddenly I see myself. I don't recognize anything here. I'm so lost I wouldn't even recognize myself. I consider returning to the place where everything still seemed to be going well, but I can't. She's taken her hand away from me. Mira, where are you? I'm the last survivor in an abandoned city, and I try to cry out her name, but my voice is higher-pitched than a human ear can hear.

6 What are these roots that clutch? What branches grow out of this stony desert? Son of man, you cannot say, because you know no more than a heap of broken images. I didn't know how long I'd roamed around the rocks of Minair. I didn't know what time it was. My watch was still on the right-hand bedside table. I was getting cold; I wished I'd put on a thicker sweater. Without wanting to accept it, I began to lose courage. I picked alleys that descended, that way I should finally come out somewhere in the lower town in a place I recognized. But each time the path began to ascend again after its original descent, or the alley ended in a square with steps that led upwards. Sometimes I got the feeling that I was going round in circles. And the bar where I'd be washed up amongst strangers I'd greet like long-lost friends who'd take me to Mira on self-navigating ships in the night, was nowhere to be seen. There wasn't a single soul on the street I could ask for directions. There wasn't anyone I could bum a cigarette off.

My attempts to walk downwards were having the opposite effect, that much was clear. So I decided to outwit the city by taking every alleyway that led upwards. I'd hit the lower part of the city as a matter of course. But the city played tricks on me once again. The ascending streets I took continued ascending. The underworld is not to be found under the earth's crust, it's high up, it's here, in Minair, in the hopeless, tobacco-less climb of these dark streets, as you're spied on by the blind windows of offensively grubby houses that are inhabited by shadows, in the compass-less rolling and turning through an exit-less labyrinth which, however much you climb, keeps sending you back over your earlier footsteps. It leads you past bizarre rock formations which rise like warts to the surface between the buildings and which, from a distance, take the form of lost loves, but they evaporate like ether as soon as you try to embrace them, and your ears ring with the inaudible sound of a dog barking and you know that there's no way back—here, in the dark of the night, obscured by the shadows of tall houses that lean threateningly towards each other above your head and the light from the rare street lamp drags your shadow behind you and then sends it rising up in front of you—here and nowhere else is the kingdom of shadows. And you know now that they've been telling you the wrong thing all this time. It is not an overcrowded, underground place where the dead wail at each other for all eternity. That would be too cozy. Neither is it a sticky-floored basement on Gregory Street, where you pay the filthy manager an *obolus* to press a button which opens a slot and gives you a view of your most lowly desires. That would be too informal. The underworld is a timeless, deserted neighborhood at night, built especially for you, which you roam about in, the last living soul in search of the most precious thing you've ever lost. In the narrow alleyways, the city only has space for a single story, and it's the one that whispers through your mind and stabs you in the guts. You can play the lyre all you like, you can levitate stones with the bewitching pain of your song, but you'll never get her back, because it is certain you'll look back—that's the nature of your longing: it is the same as that irreversible part of your past. No time exists because what you want is and will be part of what was. Panting, you climb after a remembered body, but she has sunk away behind you.

I found myself in a square I'd certainly never been in before. This had to be about the highest point of the city. There was an old, Roman church with a stubby octagonal tower. Above the main entrance there was an inscription which was still barely legible:

BEATAE VIRGINIS MINAERORUM CUSTODIS SAXORUM

This was the church of the blessed virgin of Minair, the protectress of the rocks. I was amazed that the rocks needed protection, they seemed hard enough to me, but I decided to see the mention of the rocks as a metonymy for Minair as a whole, and that solved that problem because I was already lost enough without allowing myself to get embroiled in religious and semantic difficulties. At first, I didn't see it because the alleyway was really dark, but when I did see it, a shock of recognition jolted through me. In the alley, along one side of the church, a bizarre rock formation rose up out of the pavement. This stone carbuncle had been ground flat on the top side to serve as a base for a large statue. It was the protectress of the rocks herself. There she stood in the middle of the street because the base which symbolized her protection happened to rise to the surface at this spot. She was noticeably voluptuous and was remarkably naked for a blessed virgin. To avoid any misunderstandings, the rock had been fitted with a stone plaque that identified her as the *custos saxorum* she was deemed to represent, however much, in all her monumental sensuality, she seemed more like an allegory of desire. There was no doubt about it, this was the work of Beomir van Tolo. She looked incredibly similar to Mnemosyne, The Beautiful Lady of Manora Street. He'd pulled it off again, the old rascal.

I heard voices. The noise came from somewhere in the dark alley behind the rock lady. Raise your voices in a hymn of jubilation. Finally, at long last, real living human beings in this stone jungle. Finally someone who could give me directions. Hopefully they'll have cigarettes, maybe I'll even be able to get two. I squeezed past the statue and peered into the alley. It was really dark, and I couldn't see anyone. But I could still hear noises, low voices that barked abruptly, as though commands were being issued and a peculiar, muffled noise that sounded like a child crying. I took a few steps into the alley and allowed my eyes to become accustomed to the dark. Then I saw them, in the recess of the front door of an old, dilapidated house. I saw them and I sank through the world.

7 / I saw them and they were real. In the subdued, old-fashioned darkness of the dirty alleyway they were silhouetted like actors in a black and white film. The lighting was daring, since it was as good as absent. This meant that there were no sharp contrasts, and a charming patina of charitable gray tones was laid over the scene. The pavement reflected a dark light into the night. The old, decaying façade which they'd chosen for the set provided the image with an atmospheric backdrop and it radiated a tough, whiskeyish sort of melancholy which was undeniably romantic. I could almost smell the soft, noble odor of damp, old stone and slowly rotting wood. A crack in the wall drew a powerful diagonal stroke across the focal plane. It had been put together with decidedly good taste, attention to aesthetic detail, and mood.

The actors were spread out unevenly across the focal plane. Left, seen from a ninety degree angle from behind, was a man with a long raincoat and a floppy, felt hat. He was bending over slightly. Most of his face was hidden in the shadow of the brim of his hat, giving him the air of an actor playing a tough, unapproachable romantic hero who's concealing an ink-black, painful past behind the mask of his smoky, Bourbonesque face. To the right of him moved the broad, dark back of a second man. He was also clad in black and white, wearing a raincoat of the sort that fluttered with his movements in an appropriately evasive manner. He rocked rhythmically from his hips like an actor with musicals in his blood, one who enjoyed unprecedented popularity with the female members of the audience.

Between the two long coats the features of a third man, crouched on the ground holding on to something with impressive masculine force, were visible. And what he was holding on to was the actress. She was suspended in the center of the scene by all her sighing, shimmering limbs like a breathtaking, undulating eye-catcher. Her dark dress was tugged up, torn away, and ripped in a suggestive manner. Her silvery-gray, luminous skin, which was the marble center point of the pitch black image, contrasted wonderfully with the velvet black of the dress shreds, the wide, dark-gray flapping coats, the black felt hat, and the dark shining pavement on which she lay. She shone like the moon, mirrored in the millpond-still black water of a lake at night. Her arms and legs were stretched open to each corner of the screen, as though she wanted to embrace all of the audience in the dark, smoky cinema, to comfort them and lift them up and away from their worries, from the daily grind of their dead-end struggles to make ends meet, and to transport them to a warmly lit real world where life is sweet and real and where there are happy endings. God she was beautiful.

The man behind her had laid his hand protectively over her mouth. She mewed some muffled noises, like a struggling cat. His other hand held a shining object against her creamy, silk-paper soft throat, to show her her beautiful reflection, but she kept her eyes closed because she knew she was admired and adored. The man with the hat held onto her wrists as though he were leading her in a dance. She made lovely, dramatic gestures with her hands. She had hands any actress would be jealous of: long, slender, expressive hands that were as soft as a summer's breeze, but full of character and powerful enough to throttle a swine. They were the hands of a woman who could give you everything and that could deprive you of your whole life. These hands could express everything, each one of the four hundred standard movie emotions and a hundred more, including the incredibly secret ones only the most beautiful women know about. They could paint warm colors on to a black and white canvas, and they spoke every language. These hands were her trademark and trump card. She wouldn't be able to do without them.

The rhythmically moving musicals man was busy worshipping her. He was so dazzled by her beauty that he couldn't get his fill by simply observing her. He had to touch her, and even that was not enough—he had to abolish the boundaries between himself and herself. He had to become her, impress the full length of his love into her and lose himself in her. She shuddered and crimped under his occupation. He made low, growling noises, as if adoring her was causing him pain. The two other men joined in his experience with short, panting cries of applause. Her coos vibrated softly beneath the hand on her lips. He began to dance faster and more passionately towards the finale, but the music changed and the choreography adapted itself to a new tableau before the tension could be broken. She was passed on to another dancer for a new *pas de deux*, light as a ballerina in her naked elf princess's costume. The man with the hat received her and turned her onto her stomach as if she were a most rare, breakable porcelain vase wrapped up in protective sheeting. Moonlight lit, snow-covered hills rose up from the pavement. He climbed her, covered her with his own body and became like a quilt to protect her from the cold, and he took possession of her with a firm, powerful thrust. He uttered a cry that proved that he was finally an animal, no longer a human being, and she would have backed him up with a high pitched loud scream of pleasure had the man with the knife not lovingly pressed her head to the ground. The man with the hat began to ride her as though he was galloping through the moonlight on a snow white mare, with the love of his life, over nocturnal hills, to a far-off land beyond the horizon, where they'd arrive in the morning and lie down serenely in a meadow of flowers. She was beautiful, and she turned her head sideways to sing, but before she could begin the musicals man kissed her passionately on the mouth with his abdomen. He filled her greedy mouth ever deeper and she drunk him like sweet, dark wine tasted in the evening. And once more the players redeployed themselves. The musicals man and the hat man turned her onto her back and each took care of one arm and one leg. They opened her up like an expensive folio in which the secret history of their own lives was inscribed. The other man knelt down by the lectern and afforded her the pleasure of the cool, smooth blade of his knife, which he inserted so he could carefully scrape her clean from the inside. This was too much for her. She became so ecstatic that she bit into the hand that had been lovingly laid down on her. He underlined the climax of her excitement with a full, round drum-roll on her temples. Trembling with pleasure, she let her head fall backwards onto the cushions of the ground. She was opened up still further. He licked his knife clean, laid it gently on her soft throat, climbed onto her, and began to read her with great gusto. She lay open and available, and she was a white flower in a gray world of stone. I saw her and she was beautiful. I could have invented her. I coveted her as if I'd been looking for her, and I worshipped her with my gaze as though I remembered her. And she opened her eyes, which shone through the night with the dark green stare of a predator in the jungle.

8/Rupert stood there frozen, he observed the spectacle and did nothing. Members of the jury, what did you expect? What could I have done? Which script should I have followed? I was up against superior forces. What's more they were armed. I could hardly, in a fit of perverse exhibitionism that manifested itself in a public display of courage, impetuously jump out and hit the three rapists on their backs or, like Ishida Mitsunari in the Sengoku period, bring out my pencil and unman them with three powerfully calligraphed characters that represent love. You can see the build of the defendant before you. You'll have to agree that Rupert doesn't exactly have the appearance of a street-fighter or a boxer. Where would I have found the might, or the skill, to overpower three armed men? Rupert is no Batman. I wouldn't have stood a chance. Or would you perhaps have expected me to cast my verbal capacities into the fight? To have accosted them in a friendly, yet forceful, manner, and endeavored to persuade them of the fact that it was better for their own inner peace and future as well as more beneficial to the physical and mental well being of the unfortunate girl—who, given their actions, had clearly touched their hearts—if they'd abandon the gang rape immediately and offer the victim their heartfelt apologies? Carried away as they were, they didn't particularly look like irresolute doubters who, with reason, calm, and the right arguments, could easily be persuaded to change their minds. There was a large chance that Rupert the Rescuer would have been drawn into their party game, knocked unconscious, and forced to play the role of a second victim in thanks for his plea. That kind of thing does happen, gentlemen of the jury!

I also could have withdrawn, you're right about that. I could have discretely distanced myself from the crime and I wish I had, even if it was just to spare myself having to lay down my defense before this court of justice and defend myself against the crime I'm accused of committing.

On the other hand, you'll have to acknowledge that while my inability to tear myself away may not have helped the situation, it also didn't it make it any worse. The victim would have gained nothing from my absence. Yes, I could have called the police. But do you really think I would have refrained from doing that if there had been any real possibility of reaching them? Think about it for a while! I wouldn't have been able to find the competent authorities; I didn't even know where I was. During my peregrinations through the labyrinth of Minair I'd not once been able to find a café, let alone a police station or an Alkala division army barracks. The first living souls I came across after my meeting with Dolores were those three dogs and this mangled maiden. Do you really think that if I'd gone in search of the competent authorities, at this nocturnal hour, in this abandoned stone maze, I would have suddenly bumped into hoards of inhabitants who'd kindly offer their services and point out the shortest route to the night watch's office, or let me use their mobile telephones, or, armed with pitchforks, scythes, and flails, have followed me to the place of the crime? Rupert did nothing because the hard truth was that there was nothing he could do. Worse still, doing something would only have made it worse.

Obviously I'm aware that I was a witness to one of the most disgusting and degrading crimes imaginable. And let me immediately dispel any impression that I'd in any way derived pleasure from it. Or no, I'm forced to retract that last statement. But in any case, you can't expect me to have squeezed my eyes shut, waiting, hunched up, my head in my hands, my fingers in my ears, full of disgust, until it was over. Another person might have done that, but not Rupert. The laws of the land don't require it either. And in addition to this, I could contend that, in the light of your task, it could be seen as fortunate that I persisted in my role as spectator— without my statement, you'd have had no other alternative to the factually inaccurate testimony which up to now has been given to you.

On the question of why I remained there watching, it's impossible to be brief. The simple answer is this: Rupert watches. Because that is simply what I am—a spectator. And even the most disgustingly gruesome crimes need a spectator, otherwise they've been perpetrated in vain. But this explanation is too simplistic. Her eyes were there too, through which I saw myself in the role of spectator. And there was a city that was guilty too, for she'd let me get lost in my longing, which was memory, and she'd transported the mnemonic site of my resurrection and death to a dark alleyway in Minair. And there were long coats and a felt hat that were guilty. But that's as may be, I watched and kept on watching. And whatever the precise reason was, a short circuit existed in my brain, which can be best explained with a businesslike account of the events that ensued. Members of the jury, may I ask in advance for your understanding for potential snags in my voice. It is enormously difficult for me to recount this. We've arrived at the darkest element in the charge against me.

9 They hadn't seen me. It was dark in the alley, and they were too involved in their business to keep an eye out for possible spectators. What's more, I'd taken a few steps backwards as a precaution, until I was half obscured by the base of The Beautiful Lady of the Rocks. Everything in this alley smelled of danger. And I saw her and she was as real as in a film. She had no will of her own, she was pinned down by clumsy paws, pinioned by a hairy hand, opened wide, used like a worthless object. The image of her body, her naked body, felt up, be-slobbered and possessed by brute criminality, this image was too heavy to rise up to my brains and be neutralized there. It sank directly, undiluted, to my stomach. It rushed helter skelter through my limbs. Filthy fingers wormed into her cavities. Her face was spat upon. The hat man tried with all his might to force himself into the crown of her anus. Her whole body was pain. There was a knife at her throat. She had been hit on the temples, in her stomach, and on her breasts. The musicals man forced her mouth open with his hand and thrust his penis in as far as her uvula. I saw it happen before my eyes. Mira lay there, sticky with pounding man-sweat, and she trembled with pleasure, like defenseless prey being torn apart. Her death scream shuddered through my body. It happened in my stomach and it spread through my limbs.

She looked at me, and I saw myself through her eyes. I was playing a part in her film. I coveted her, I possessed her with my staring gaze. I couldn't do anything about it. It sunk away from my stomach and took hold of me. It spread unstoppably. My pants pinch. I have a hard on. Rupert sees Mira and has a real hard erection in his own stiff flesh and blood dick, as hard as a rock. Before my eyes I see her arch her moaning body. Look, Mira, look what you do to me. I undo my pants, and my cock springs out like a young fighting bull. The knife man claws her, spreads his fingers in her hair, and pulls her into his lap, like he's sticking the head of a captured slave on a stake as a trophy. The musicals man hits her on her chin and bites into her tits. The hat man pulls her thighs apart as if he wants to tear her apart, setting free his thick-witted lust with violent jabs into the intimate door to her soul, and I can't do anything. I can't stop myself. She looks at me like an animal. I see myself with her eyes. Tear me, tigress, possess me with your nails and teeth. Stop it, she says. But she doesn't want me to stop. Look, Mira, look at me. I'm doing it. You are being brutally raped by three unknown men and I'm rubbing myself off. You've got the glowing rod of Benno, with his pretentious poet's coat and his ridiculous felt hat and his oh so fabulously interesting fake poet fake friends, in your sopping cunt, and I'm standing by watching, and I'm rubbing my own cock those horny cocks in your horny cunt, your horny mouth and your horny ass. Filthy bastard, she says, but she only says that because she wants me to go on. Look at me as you fuck someone else. Give me your hand, feel how hard my love is for you. I love you, Mira, dear, dear Mira. I love you so much. Look what I'm doing for you. I'm worshipping you. I'm adoring the astonishing beauty of your body, which is allowing itself to be used by these three dogs at the same time. I'll make a sacrifice to you Mira, my sugar-sweet, shimmering Mira. I'll give you what you've always wanted. Look at me. It's coming. It's just for you Mira, Mira, look, Mira.

And she looked at me with wide open eyes, and they showed more bewilderment and despair than the eyes of a hundred sailors, windjammers set and sailing at full speed off the edge of the world, sailors who knew that there wasn't a single possibility of escaping an eternal fall into the deepest darkness of the void. And the exact instant I came, she fell, escaping into the deep, dark falling that is unconsciousness. They hadn't noticed a thing, those bastards. They pounded into her lifeless body as if it were a leaky sandbag. All the openings had been tried out, and now they were being tested again in different positions. There was no end to it. There was no compassion in their actions. And Rupert the Unrescuable stood there, turning to stone, stuck in the no-man's-land of unprocessed awareness of what was happening and what he'd done, his hand still on his semi-erect penis and sperm on his fingers, on his pants, and on the shiny, black pavement of the alleyway. And she didn't look at me anymore, and I was empty. Not a single thought occurred to me, despite a far-off dormant suspicion that the thoughts that would present themselves would bore into me like ice-picks.

There was a sudden barking, not far away. The three rapists were frozen in surprise. And again. A malicious dog. It seemed even closer by than before. It was a raw, angry noise that tore into this abandoned neighborhood like a chainsaw. The men clearly didn't feel like taking this on. It should stay a bit of fun. They could do without bumping into a large dog in their current state. And where there's a dog there's usually people. They hurriedly pulled themselves free of her, stood up, and made off at great speed away from the church square, deeper into the dark alley. They left their beloved behind on the street like a deflated blow-up doll. I just glimpsed them trying to do up their clothes as they ran, and then they disappeared into the darkness. I heard their footsteps fade away into the night.

I stood there, frozen. She lay on that dirty pavement, a few meters from me, naked, raped, mutilated, and unconscious. No dog came. I didn't hear any more barking either. There was a deathly silence. It was the most silent silence that can exist. I don't know how long I stood there, turned to stone behind the base of the statue of the protectress of the rocks. I was in no state to think or to move. Time didn't exist. She lay there and I saw her.

Finally, I came to. I did up my pants, came out from behind the statue, and walked towards her. The sight of her tore me apart. She'd been broken. I kneeled down beside her. With both hands, I carefully picked her up off the pavement. She was as light as a dead cat. I had to cover her up, she'd get cold. Her own clothes, tossed around everywhere, were unusable. They were torn to tatters. I had nothing to warm her up with. I wished I'd put on a thicker sweater. I sat on the ground and took her in my arms. I embraced her as gently as I could. Hush now, darling, I'm here. I'm holding you. I softly stroked her cheek, her hair, and her hand.

I don't know how long I sat there. There was no time. I sat there and I just sat there and I held a strange, unfamiliar body in my arms. If I could cry, I would have cried then.

The rest—the passing night courier, being given the black eyes, the ambulance, the police, and the arrest—is sufficiently known to you.

10 Most venerable members of the jury, that is my truthful and faithful account of the events that took place on the Sunday, April 13th, in question.

She wasn't Mira. I know that. The unfortunate victim, referred to as Karin H. in the case file, was completely unknown to me. Nevertheless she was Mira because I wanted her to be. Mira is the essence of everything. My actions depended on her, my defense depends on her, my life depends on her. She is the city I lost myself in. That I haven't succeeded in having her appear before you as a chief witness, as my motive and my motivation, my lawyer and my head prosecutor, the harsh jailer in my Miralessness incarceration, my martyrdom and my masochism, my sugar-sweet, shimmering Mira, is a circumstance which I lament more than you, believe me. If she'd appeared before you today, she would have corroborated my account, absolved me from blame, and set me free. That the Office of Public Prosecution hasn't been able to track her down doesn't surprise me, to be honest. But she is real, I swear it, my God she's real. She is as real as the person who stands before you, she is as real as the city I've traversed so many times, including the Sunday in question, and she is as real as a dream become reality. She is the fact that makes fiction impossible.

I know I will never find her again. My only hope is that she will read about the Court case in the newspapers. Perhaps some journalist will include a brief mention of the leading role she has played in the defendant's atement. There's a slight chance that she'll go to the trouble of applying ̇he Clerk's Department for the minutes of this sitting. Then she'll ̇ the record of my witness statement, and she will read as I read the ̇n the April 13th in question, and she will read that I read nothing ̇er in the city. Mira, I cry out your name and my voice is higher than a human ear can hear. Read this. Read me and read how I got lost in the city which reminded me of you and longed for you with all of its streets, squares, churches, cafés, monuments, and statues. Read the city and read how it is the memory site of my longing for you. Read this and read yourself because you are my only story. The city, my travels, and this journey through my memory, which is also longing, are made legible by the sunshine of your dark green eyes. I can't go to the sea without your dark green eyes. Be Mira again, Mira, and find me.

Ladies and gentlemen of the jury, I ask your forgiveness. That outburst was inadmissible. I wouldn't want to give even the slightest impression that I'd abused this austere Court by using the proceedings to win back my greatest loss. That would demonstrate an intolerable scorn for the seriousness of my case and the rectitude you embody. I let myself go. Although that is no excuse, perhaps I can offer the explanation for my lapse and argue that the whole matter discussed today does not leave me entirely unmoved. But it won't happen again. I apologize, and in my continuation, the short continuation remaining to us, I will limit myself to the points that are relevant to my crime, or alleged crime, as set down in the charge.

In the charge only one suspect is mentioned. Just one single rapist. This is in contradiction to the facts. There were definitely three. I swear it under oath. Besides it not being true, it's also not very likely that there was just one rapist involved in the crime. Because if that had been the case, I could have, despite my build, certainly attempted to overpower him. My inability to undertake such a thing proves that I was outnumbered.

To my regret, I can't give you any useful description of the three men I saw commit the crime. It was a dark night, and the alleyway where the crime took place is located in a dark neighborhood, and within this neighborhood the alleyway in question is a relatively dark one. My observation post, half hidden behind the base of the statue of the blessed virgin of Minair, lady protectress of the rocks, gives a good enough view of the events to be able to be certain that my account is in complete alignment with the facts, but it was set too far back from the scene of the crime to observe the details necessary for a reliable description, beyond the rough indication that all three of them looked like Benno, particularly the man with the floppy felt hat. In addition, there was the matter of the hat rim that created a dark shadow over a face and the raincoats which flapped shapelessly and hid their builds.

I'm aware that the prosecutor's reconstruction of events is based on the explicit and unambiguous witness statement of the victim. I've no explanation as to why Karin H.'s testimony runs counter to the facts. Of course we shouldn't doubt the integrity of her intentions for a moment—if someone can benefit from giving you a completely true version of the events of the last Sunday April 13th then it is she—and it seems we can rule out her having twisted the facts to show me in a bad light. If she talks about a single rapist, then it's because she remembers a single rapist, that's what we should assume. But without wanting to give the impression of being a specialist in the area of the psychological aftereffects of a rape, I do want you to consider that there are documented incidences of the victims of extremely violent crimes and sexual offenses who, during the process of an unconscious repression, come to terms with the unbearable gravity of the crime by remembering it as less terrible than it really was. The fact that her description of the supposed one, single rapist matches my appearance and bodily attributes must be the consequence of a similar dark mechanism in the machinery of her memory. And you must realize that she did actually see me. She looked at me. I was the last thing she saw before she fell unconscious.

On the one hand, you've got my infallible memory; on the other, the understandable distortions of her tortured memory. I find the suggestion that Rupert might be a fabulist, present as spurious innuendo and a distinct undercurrent of defamation in the oral pleadings of my prosecutor, very unsettling. This cheap and vulgar accusation, which he was nowhere able to corroborate in his arguments, and which he never once dared to explicitly pronounce—which really says enough already, members of the jury—was obviously meant to influence your perception of my account in indecent ways, by sowing nagging doubts about my honesty and about my intentions and capacity to limit myself to the facts, before I'd even spoken my first word. I emphatically deny this bogus accusation. Rupert s no fantasist. My account is as real as this city. I've talked as I've taken ou with me on a tour of the city past the sites of my memory. The words have pronounced are the words I meant to pronounce because they are immured, carved, and riveted in the walls and monuments of the city. The events these words describe are the events I remember. This memory is infallible, and these events are the events that took place, because they, just as my argument, are anchored in the route I set down and because they, just as my argument, are interwoven with the stories the city has to tell. I read these stories in the streets and squares. I listen to the memories the statues whisper. I see the stories in the gestures of passers-by. I know this city. I read her like a beloved's face and I do not invent her.

Which brings us to the issue of the DNA investigation. I have no explanation as to why no traces of the DNA of the three men who had the rape on their consciences was found on the victim's body. Indeed, one would expect sweat, skin cells, hair, and nail dirt to have been left behind on her skin. Perhaps an explanation can be sought in the fact that the three men were dressed in raincoats, made from a type of fabric that doesn't shed, and that they didn't bare any more of their bodies than was strictly necessary for their deeds. That not even the tiniest trace of their sperm was found is, on the contrary, clear confirmation of the truth of my account. We needn't doubt for a second that this substance would have been found in abundance if they hadn't broken off from their crime prematurely because of the barking dog, which for that matter shouldn't shorten the sentence served for their hideous act, but I don't need to tell you that.

As the prosecutor has strongly emphasized—and this is something I have every understanding for, it's his duty to do this—there was sperm on the victim's body which had the same DNA structure as the samples taken from me for the trial. I'd like to remind you for that matter that I've been totally cooperative towards your investigations. This discovery doesn't not make my case any rosier, on first sight, I'll admit it. The explanation is nevertheless simple. When, in that dark alleyway in Minair which under the eyes of The Beautiful Lady changed into Manora Street, when I, in my state of diminished responsibility, my Mira drunkenness, in a film which was the film of my resurrection and death, in the most painful minutes of my painful life, jerked off at the sight, at seeing, at seeing Mira raped by three men, and saw myself with her eyes, that I jerked off by watching her be raped, the women who was the most precious thing I'd ever lost, brutally raped by three men, and it wasn't her but it was her, because I wanted it to be, and I jerked off—Forgive me. I'll pick up again. It's difficult, I'll try to stick to the facts. I jerked off as I watched this repulsive scene. This deed, at which I blush more deeply than I can say, but which at the time filled me with deep, dark green, bristling pleasure, was successful in the sense that the desired result was reached. There was the matter of an orgasm accompanied by a release of sperm. During the confusing moments that followed I've no precise notion of where the ejaculation reached, but we can safely assume that my guilt stuck to more places than just my pants and the pavement of that Minair alleyway—but that it also soiled my hand. Members of the jury, I had sperm on my fingers. And after the hasty departure of the three rapists, I used these fingers to pick up the poor, unconscious victim from the cold street, embraced her, warmed her up, consoled her, and caressed her.

The prosecutor would have you believe that my guilt concerning the act I've been charged of, may be proven by my character and personality. He'd have Rupert calculating and base. He'd be capable of anything because he was confident that his intelligence would get him out of any awkward situation. The prosecutor flatters me. And I must admit that I do understand many things better than other people, significantly better in fact, but I'm not aware of committing any punishable offense by this. And he'd have Rupert a sexist. This accusation which the prosecutor labored long over—he deserves nothing but praise for the brilliant ways in which he has peppered his charge with references to my base desires, and for the wily rhetoric of humor and disgust with which he has tried to reduce me to a copulator of the worst sort, who'll sink to anything, to an underbelly character and perpetrator of crime, in particular his passage about the wandering hands which lapped at The Corona di Mócani waitress's curves like panting puppies—was a masterly specimen of rhetorical manipulation. This man understands his job, I'll generously hand him that. This accusation was, of course, to be expected given the nature of the transgression I've been accused of. I have every faith that this accusation has been dispatched and disproved by my account of the facts. If Rupert was a sexist, he wouldn't be such an energetic one.

Rupert is not Karin H.'s rapist. The principal reason that Rupert can hardly be guilty of the act he's been accused of is Mira. She is, as I untiringly go on emphasizing and now for the final time with the most possible stress repeat, the essence of my case. She proves my innocence. Because it was her. It was she who was raped by three men in a dark alleyway in Minair on the Sunday night of April 13th this year. I know that it wasn't her but it was her too. I wanted it to be her. I'd spent the entire day walking past the memory sites of my longing for her. I'd paused for a long time in front of the second floor apartment of Number 15 of the alley with the improbable name where I'd won her, and in Manora Street, where I'd lost her; I'd even involuntarily looked up to a window on the second floor. I'd seen her Polish and pliant in Gregory Street. I set foot on the stage of Fredo Square with her on my arm, and, on the terrace of The Raven, I'd written the novel of the city with her and we'd done some mind-fucking. I'd seen her sitting there like a woman in the mirrors of her sparklingly decorated favorite local. And I'd looked for her and I'd got lost in her body. And when I saw her in that black and white alley, with hair that must have been red and the dark green predators that were her eyes, it was her, it had to be her, it couldn't be anyone but her.

Most venerable members of the jury, how in God's name could I have raped Mira? She was my dream incarnate. She was all the women I'd imagined and had worshipped a thousand times, and she was seven times seven more beautiful than them, and she was real. She was the fact that made fiction impossible. And in all her unparalleled reality she shrunk me like a prophet at the sight of an angel. She could only erect me once I could dream her up before my eyes like a shimmering mirage. Only then could my longing become flesh, when I played a part as I've always played, when I play the role of audience in her film, and when I see myself in my role and see myself being observed with her eyes. That evening in the Minair alleyway, watched by The Lady of the Rocks, I played a role in the same film as previously for The Beautiful Lady of Manora Street. I could be a man because I saw her being abused by three dogs, like in a film, and through her eyes I saw myself watching. But tell me, most venerable ladies and gentlemen of the jury, tell me in all sincerity: How would I, Rub-off Rupert, with my so profoundly cursed incapacity, finding her real, marble body in my own violent hands, have been capable, in God's name, of persuading my body, my worthless, disobedient, impotent body, to do what it precisely failed to do when faced with her, the angel who descended in the shape of an angel and who promised to deliver me eternally from my dreams?

Rupert is a spectator, not an actor. Rupert reads the city in the face of his beloved. Rupert doesn't act. Spectating is the only way to take part. If that's his crime, he pleads guilty.

The defendant rests his case.

Ilja Leonard Pfeijffer is a poet, novelist, literary critic, and former Ancient Greek scholar at Leiden University. The winner of numerous prizes—he's the only Dutch author to have won both of the most coveted debut poetry and prose prizes in the Netherlands—Pfeijffer is the editor of the literary journal *De Revisor* and founder and editor of the poetry journal *Awater*. *Rupert: A Confession* is his first novel to be translated into English.

M ichele Hutchison studied literature and languages at the Universities of East Anglia and Cambridge in England before taking a job in publishing. She worked at various British publishing houses before moving to Amsterdam, where she works as a translator and editor. In addition to Ilja Leonard Pfeijffer, she has translated the Dutch novelist Simone van der Vlugt and the journalist Joris Luyendijk.

Open Letter—the University of Rochester's nonprofit, literary translation press—is one of only a handful of publishing houses dedicated to increasing access to world literature for English readers. Publishing twelve titles in translation each year, Open Letter searches for works that are extraordinary and influential, works that we hope will become the classics of tomorrow.

Making world literature available in English is crucial to opening our cultural borders, and its availability plays a vital role in maintaining a healthy and vibrant book culture. Open Letter strives to cultivate an audience for these works by helping readers discover imaginative, stunning works of fiction and by creating a constellation of international writing that is engaging, stimulating, and enduring.

Current and forthcoming titles from Open Letter include works from Argentina, Catalonia, France, Germany, Iceland, Russia, and numerous other countries.

www.openletterbooks.org